KELLYANNE

by Daniel T. Willis, Sr.

DORRANCE PUBLISHING CO
EST. 1920
PITTSBURGH, PENNSYLVANIA 15238

Dorrance Publishing Co
585 Alpha Drive
Pittsburgh, PA 15238
Visit our website at *www.dorrancebookstore.com*

ISBN: 979-8-88812-411-6
eISBN: 979-8-88812-911-1

KELLYANNE

Table of Contents

Acknowledgements

To the incredible staff at Dorrance Publishing, whose unparalleled efforts in the areas of copyediting, cover design, publication, promotion and distribution brought this endeavor from hope to fruition. And to my Project Manager, Taryn Wells, whose expertise in coordinating all aspects of the process while keeping me well-informed I want to express my eternal gratitude and utmost appreciation. Thank you, Taryn, for your leadership, guidance, and professionalism!

Dedication

This book is dedicated first and foremost to God, The Father, who after catastrophic complications during brain surgery that should have left me in a near vegetative state, fully restored my neurological capabilities and gave me an unexpected capacity for creativity that I never had before. Secondly, I dedicate this book to my wife of 22 years, Marissa, whose willingness to sacrifice time we could have spent together made this dream of mine possible.

CHAPTER

ONE

The Bronx. Land of the fee. Home of the depraved. Migrants and immigrants paid dearly for having dreams and aspirations of a better life. The stigma attached to the region labeled its inhabitants far from complimentary. Half-empty buses drove high school students to facilities many would fail to graduate from. More than half the population lived at high or extreme poverty levels.

It was a borough of hills and flatlands, irregular streets, tenements and housing developments, bridges, tunnels, buses, subways and trains. Overcrowded, with a minority majority, devastated by arson, insurance fraud, gang violence, and poverty. Residents woke up every morning, traveling from east and west-named streets divided on either side by Jerome Avenue, heading for jobs that sustained their meager existence. They shopped at Fordham Road, Bay Plaza, The Hub, Bruckner Road, and Riverdale/Kingsbridge Shopping Center. "Bronx Week" offered an annual respite, with festivities celebrated in different ways to accommodate cultural diversity. And, of course, there was the galvanizing effect of Yankee Stadium, with the ever-present hope of another pennant or trip to the World Series. Every household lived in a world of its own that best suited the needs of that particular family.

Marianne Summers, an out-of-work hairstylist, stretched across her side of the unstable mahogany sleigh bed for the cubed box of Kleenex on the nightstand. After plucking five of them, she sat up and bent over to empty the whiskey-tainted contents of her compassionate mouth. She dropped the used wad of paper into a miniature bamboo wastebasket, then laid on her back, patted her husband, Jerome, a taxi driver for South Bronx Transportation, three times gently on the chest, and rolled to her left side. Jerome closed his mouth, opened his eyes, and looked at her.

"Honey," he said softly, "You didn't have to do that."

No reply.

"Marianne?" He nudged her gently.

She turned and smiled. "I wanted to… You have needs… I know that, dear."

"But you're not well… I can take a step back."

Marianne sat up on her right elbow. "You shouldn't have to," she said. "I'm supposed to be there for you. It's really not a problem."

"But doesn't it cause you discomfort?"

"No. Why do you ask?"

"You know," he said, raising both arms to form an "L" at his chest. "The crumpled body posture. Doesn't that get tedious in your condition?"

Marianne's eyes narrowed. "My *condition*?"

"Yeah, you know…This predicament…"

She lowered her right hand, made a fist, and punched her pillow. She shifted back to her left side.

"What did I say?" said Jerome, leaning toward her. "I'm just trying to let you know I understand, honey…"

She began to sob openly.

"Come on, Marianne," he said, reaching for her right shoulder. "What did I do? What do you want me to say? Don't cry…"

Marianne tossed his hand away, moved toward him and onto her knees. She straddled his lap, wiped the tears from her eyes, and cupped his high cheekbones in both hands.

"I do not have a *condition*," she said in a low, steady tone of voice. "*We* do not have a *predicament*… I want you to call it what it is… *Cervical cancer!*" She shook his face twice. "Say it, Bucky! Stage IV c*ervical cancer!*"

"*Cervical cancer…*" he said, finding it difficult to maintain composure.

His eyes watered. He covered her trembling hands with his own as they sat nose-to-nose…

Time passed. One Friday night, four years later, Marianne hugged her girls at the polished walnut rectangular dining room table and sent them off to bed. She glanced at the used grandfather clock against the west wall. With the left hand, she rubbed her forehead, wrapping the right arm around her waist. Minutes later, her overworked taxi driver stumbled through the front door. His overcoat and high-collared white shirt were disheveled, squinting with bloodshot eyes, as he took four steps, stopped, and looked at her.

"Stopped by Stan's Sports Bar on the way home again, I take it?" she said, with pursed lips.

Jerome exhaled, choosing not to reply. He walked over to her, pulled a chair from the table and sat down.

Marianne extended her right arm to place a gentle hand on his left wrist. "Bucky," she said. "We have to do something. Need to talk about this, dear…"

Bucky sat listening as she laid out a list of possible solutions. It would take a year to formulate a plan of action he could get on board with.

CHAPTER

TWO

Ten-year-old Nellyanne Summers sat up on the narrow, Rosewood twin bed, knees raised, arms wrapped around her shins, determined to get what was rightfully hers. The aluminum-based nightlight on an old-fashioned reading desk nearby captured just enough of her polyester pajama-clad body for him to know she was there. At dinner, earlier that evening, Mommy announced Daddy's desire to say goodnight to his twin daughters before they went to sleep. The girls would rotate every other night, with Mommy deciding the first visit would go to Kellyanne.

But Nellyanne was the oldest—albeit by only six minutes. *She* should be the first to receive a visit! God only knows, Kellyanne already received the lion share of his affection. After reading *Curious George*—a story that always put the favored twin to sleep—Nellyanne took Kellyanne's yellow hair ribbon from under her sister's pillow, replacing it with her blue one, and headed for the guestroom.

Nellyanne and Kellyanne were more than just twins. They were identical and indistinguishable to everyone but Mommy and Daddy—that is, when Daddy wasn't drinking. Mommy came up with the idea of colored hair ribbons—leftover from Christmas wrappings—to make life easier for family, friends, neighbors, and teachers. The girls would often entertain themselves by switching ribbons, and watching others struggle mightily to tell them apart. Mommy would laugh until abdominal pain made the effort unbearable…

Staggering footsteps approached the pine wood door. The rusted hinges squeaked loudly as it opened. Daddy took one step forward, two backward, then stood in the doorway.

"Kelly?"

"Yes, Daddy. It's me…See?" She leaned toward the nightlight to reveal the ribbon. He smiled broadly.

"There's my little girl! Did Mommy tell you I wanted to see you tonight?"

"Yes, sir. She said you wanted to say goodnight."

"That's right. But first, I have something for you."

He brought his right arm around, holding a brown paper bag.

"What is that, Daddy?"

"Well, let's see…"

He stumbled to the bed, sat down, and opened the bag. He pulled out a sixteen-ounce container of Borden's Butter Brickle ice cream and a small wooden spoon. Nellyanne raised both hands to her mouth. She jumped to throw her arms around his neck. The stench of Wild Irish Rose Whiskey was almost unbearable, but she didn't care.

"Thank you, Daddy! Thank you, thank you, thank you!" She sat down, pulled back the tab, and grabbed the spoon. Within minutes, she'd eaten one-third of the tub.

"Whoa there, little girl," he said, taking the spoon from her hand. "You'll have a stomachache and won't be able to sleep tonight."

She nodded and smiled. He reached for the container, fumbled to re-seal it, then sat it on the desk with the spoon. He turned to put his left arm around her shoulders. She lowered her head to his lap.

"You're right, Daddy," she said. "I'll finish it tomorrow…"

He began to run his fingers through her curly black hair. "You know you're Daddy's favorite, right?" he said. "Parents are not supposed to say that, but I can't help it. There was always something special about you, Kelly. Do you know what that is?"

"No, sir…" She rolled over, resting the back of her head in his lap.

"You were always the one I could depend on. The way you look forward to the time we spend together. I feel like you would do anything for me if I asked."

"Oh, I would, Daddy! Absolutely anything!"

"Then you should know… Daddy needs you now…"

THREE

"What is it, Daddy?"

"Do you know the meaning of the word 'stress'?"

"No…"

"Stress is what you feel when you work hard all day, but barely make enough money to take care of your family—your wife—your girls… It rips you apart inside."

"Is it like a disease?"

"Sort of…"

"Why don't you go to a doctor, then?"

"Don't have the money right now, Kelly. Doctors can't cure it, anyway."

"Who can cure it?"

"Well… You can, dear…"

"Me? How?"

"With love… Love is what cures it. Love will make it go away… Your love, Kelly…"

Nellyanne jumped up and sat upright on the side of the bed. She placed both hands on his left thigh.

"Then I will cure it, Daddy! I'll make it go away right now! Where is it? In your head? Your chest? Your legs?"

"It's actually between my legs…" he said, standing to face her. "It's in here…"

Nellyanne waited anxiously while his belt buckle opened, and the zipper came down. She wanted desperately to cure her father. Her eyes widened when his pants and briefs dropped to the laminated wood floor.

"Do you know what this is, dear?"

"It…It looks like a snake sleeping between two rocks in a sack, Daddy…"

Jerome laughed. "This is Daddy's penis," he said. "The stress is inside of it…"

Nellyanne looked closer. Her eyes squinted. "What do I do, Daddy?" she said. "How do I make it come out?"

"You put your palm, thumb, and fingers around it," he directed. "Then you pull it back and forth… You know, like milking a cow… Here, I'll show you…"

He took her right hand, placed it on his member, adjusted her fingers, and demonstrated the proper motion. She was a quick study, giggling at the way it moved like a squishy toy, poking in and out through her semi-circular grip.

"This is fun, Daddy!" she exclaimed. "You'll be cured in no time!"

He smiled and looked up at the ceiling; eyes closed.

"That's it, dear…Just like that…Ooooohhhh…"

Suddenly, she gasped and stopped stroking. Daddy looked down with open eyes.

"What's wrong, dear? Why did you stop?"

"It's changing, Daddy! Getting bigger…hard…angry! I don't think it likes what I'm doing!"

"No, that's normal, dear," he said, moving strands of loose hair behind her left ear. "Just means the cure is working. Keep going, precious…"

"Okay…" she whispered.

"That's my girl. Now do it a bit faster… Yes… Like that… Ooooohhhh."

Nellyanne noticed another change in the snake's appearance. "Daddy," she said. "The top part of it is turning purple!"

"That's normal, too, sweetheart. It means we need to do something else now."

"What?" she said, as it seemed to grow bigger, more menacing, with every stroke. She imagined, any minute now, it would leap from her grasp, lash out and bite her on the nose!

"Open your mouth," he said. "Use it along with your hand… Suck it with a back and forth motion… Like you would a popsicle…"

He reached for her chin to guide her to his now pulsating erection.

Picturing her second favorite treat—only warm, with a lavender top—made it easier to make the necessary transition. Taking nearly three-quarters of it into her mouth, Nellyanne moved with the precision of a well-paid hooker. She sensed the need to go faster as Daddy's legs stiffened.

"Oh yes!" he groaned. "That's it! Here comes the stress, Kelly… It's going to shoot out into your mouth… Keep moving your head and hand like that… Yes… DON'T PANIC… JUST SWALLOW… NOW!"

She felt the powerful spurts splash over her tongue and down her throat. She couldn't swallow fast enough, as stress spilled down her chin and onto her pajama top. She wiped her mouth and chest afterward, then looked up at him.

"Did it work, Daddy? Are you cured?"

With wobbly knees, he reached down to caress her left cheek. "Yes, dear. You did well. Daddy feels much better now…"

She smiled… and belched.

Daddy left the room first, taking the ice cream with him. Nellyanne heard the faint sounds of him murmuring something to Mommy as he opened and closed the refrigerator. She waited for a few moments for silence before opening the door. Mommy sat at the dining room table, staring off into space. The hinges squealed, as Nellyanne pulled the knob behind her. Mommy never looked her way…

CHAPTER

FOUR

Nights turned into weeks, months, then years. Kellyanne no longer felt the guilt of waking up every other morning, believing she'd missed another visit with Daddy. She eventually outgrew the nightly readings with her sister, along with the "childish" desire to say goodnights to her father, apart from Mommy. After middle school, homework became the primary focus, as any chance of a college education depended on an academic scholarship. She studied nightly to the point of exhaustion, falling asleep immediately afterward. Nellyanne shared her sister's intellectual enthusiasm but continued the charade of visits in secret.

On nights designated for Kellyanne, sexual encounters with Daddy came to be more about saving Mommy and Daddy's marriage than relieving stress. Daddy took Nellyanne's virginity at age fifteen, he explained, to spare her the pain and humiliation she would suffer if he left such a delicate task to "some bumbling, inexperienced idiot." They used condoms. As an added precaution, she received Depo-Provera shots. He taught her to give and receive oral sex, the art of masturbation, a plethora of *Kama Sutra* positions, how to work around periods, and introduced her to the first of many orgasms.

One night, down the hall and a world away, Kellyanne awakened suddenly from a restless sleep. Her pulse was racing. She found it difficult to breathe. Inexplicably, she felt as if her body was being moved around the top bunk. She leaned over the side and peered at the empty bed below. Across the room, the bathroom door was open, dark and empty.

Marianne, as with all nights assigned to her younger twin, sat quietly at the dining room table. She seemed startled when the bedroom door opened. She closed her lavender and white, terrycloth robe and whisked loose strands of hair behind each ear.

"Hi, Mommy," said a groggy Kellyanne.

"Hello, dear," said Marianne, dabbing each eyelid with a Kleenex tissue. "What's wrong? Can't sleep?"

"No, I'm fine, Mommy," said Kellyanne, approaching the table. "Where's Nellyanne? She wasn't in her bunk when I woke up. I found this under my pillow…"

Where's Nellyanne? The words shook Marianne from a haze of contemplation into the reality of to whom she was actually speaking.

Her mouth opened when she saw the blue ribbon in Kellyanne's open palm. Her face turned pale. She raised both hands to her mouth and gasped out loud. Leaning to the right of her obviously duped daughter, Marianne glared at the guestroom door.

"What's wrong, Mommy?" Kellyanne said, following the line of her mother's gaze.

Without answering, Mommy stood, turned and ran into the master bedroom, slamming the door behind her.

FIVE

Nellyanne repositioned herself on all fours, face buried into the pillow to muffle her screams. Daddy groaned loudly, as the pace of his thrusts quickened. His penis hardened in final preparation. Nellyanne lifted her head and looked left.

"I feel it, Daddy! But don't cum yet… I want to see it! Taste it! Pull it out, Daddy… NOW!"

He did, unsheathed the ribbed protector, and began to pump vigorously. Nellyanne whirled around to face it, moved his hand, lunged forward and swallowed it whole. Daddy's violent scream made it impossible to hear the whining of the door…

Nellyanne continued to suck with full intent to milk him dry. Losing containment, temporarily, as he softened and collapsed over her left shoulder, she quickly gobbled him up again as he shivered with every gulp. She sat up afterward, pinched each corner of her mouth, and giggled as he fell into a coma-like sleep. Only then did she notice the pajama-clad mirror image standing just a few feet away.

"Kellyanne?" she said with raised eyebrows. Her twin stood rigid, both hands to mouth, with bloodshot eyes.

"How long have you been there?" Nellyanne said, quickly shifting both legs to the side of the bed, placing her feet firmly on the floor. She paused, reached for her pajama top, put it on, and began buttoning it.

Kellyanne refused to answer.

Nellyanne looked at her father, threw the blanket over his lap, and looked back at Kellyanne. She was gone. The blue ribbon and bobby pin attachment lay crumpled on the floor where she'd been standing...

Back in the bedroom, Kellyanne climbed the ladder and fell onto her bunk in tears. She cried and cried, rolling around on the bed.

She laid on her back and began to pummel the mattress while flailing her legs, until she stopped suddenly to scream at the top of her lungs, "NOOOOOOOOO! YOU BITCH! MOTHER FUCKING BITCH!!"

She took three deep breaths. Calming somewhat, she searched desperately for a mental image to replace the one she'd just witnessed. South Bronx High... Chemistry homework... The constant smell of marijuana coming from Mrs. Delarosa's living room window... The taste and texture of butter brickle ice cream... Tommy Borders... Tommy!

She'd met her first crush, a farm hand, last year while visiting her grandparents on Daddy's side in Boise, Idaho. He was tall with a tanned complexion, a full head of cherry blonde hair. His smile was mesmerizing, as he watched her talk with Grandpa on the front porch while leaning against a cherry tree in the front yard of the house next door... It was love at first sight.

When Grandpa stepped inside the screen door to fetch them both a glass of strawberry iced tea, she turned to find Tommy standing there. He'd climbed the cyclone fence to meet her.

"Hi. I'm Tommy...Tommy Borders," he said. "I work for the Bedfords next door... You from around here?"

He smiled broadly, tilting his head slightly forward and to the left in the cutest way, she thought. Kellyanne pretended not to notice the warmth of his eyes on the breast pockets of her tight petti-blouse. Her love of art made her appreciate the way his V-shaped upper torso poured into his waist with perfect symmetry. Hips that bowed slightly outward, highlighted two magnificently carved, sturdy legs she could see bulging through the dark blue overalls.

"Kellyanne Summers," she said. "And no, I'm from New York... South Bronx. We're visiting my grandparents for the summer."

Just then, Grandpa walked out with two tall glass tumblers. He handed one to Kellyanne and looked at Tommy.

"Hey there, young man!" he said. "I see you've met one of my grand-daughters. Beauty, ain't she?" he said, placing his left hand on her right shoulder.

"Please, Gramps!" Kellyanne exclaimed. "You're embarrassing me! And thank you. This looks delicious." She took the tumbler and smiled.

Tommy folded his arms and nodded. "She sure is, sir," he said. "Very much so. In fact, she's the prettiest thing I've seen around here yet!"

While thoughts of Tommy cleared her mind of recent memory, the imagery also stirred up feelings of an ill-fated erotic encounter. Kellyanne clenched her thighs to temper the surge of mounting pressure between her legs. She remembered the day her country crush convinced her to come with him to the red barn in the neighbors' backyard. The Bedfords weren't home, and Nellyanne was at the produce market with Ninny and Gramps, so the timing seemed perfect. She was nervous, but smitten and willing. At nearly sixteen, to finally put an end to her status as a virgin.

"Will it hurt, Tommy?" she said, with both hands on his bare chest, as they lay in a soft, crunchy bed of hay.

"I don't think so," he said, breathing heavily. "It's not very big."

"I want to see it first," she said, pushing herself up on both elbows.

Tommy leaned back on his knees. He held the shaft with his right hand, as the bulbous, pink head peered outward. She stared momentarily, took a deep breath, then laid back down.

"Okay," she said quietly, spreading her legs. "Gently now... Slowly, Tommy..."

"I will..." He leaned forward and aimed for an area he'd only fantasized about.

As soon as the head of his penis touched her pubic hair, he screamed and collapsed, falling on his back to her left. Kellyanne watched the lively spurts of semen shoot from its tip, come back down, and coat the shaft. Suddenly, she sprang to her feet, pulled up her panties, and ran out of the drafty barn. Tommy just laid there, eyes closed, mouth open, shaking sporadically. They never spoke again.

With eyes closed, Kellyanne laid on the top bunk ten months later, wondering if she would indeed die a virgin. She grabbed a handful of pajama bottom material between her legs. She saw Tommy: his smile, the bulbous head of his erection, felt the anticipation of penetration, the flow of his semen… Daddy's penis: its length and girth after shedding the condom; the way it disappeared into Nellyanne's mouth. The quick, frantic back and forth motion of her head; the look in Daddy's eyes before he came—the look in Tommy's eyes immediately afterward…

Meanwhile, her right hand had stealthily found its way inside the elastic waist band. She shuddered when fingers lightly brushed her genitalia. From memory, they worked in rhythm—slowly, then faster and faster—until she had to use her left palm to smother the scream of an intense orgasm. She lay heaving for several minutes before curling up into a fetal position.

CHAPTER

SIX

Ambient lighting from the hallway traced a path along the carpeted floor to the small computer desk on the left and one half of the bunk bed on the right. Nellyanne walked over to the desk, removed the yellow ribbon from her hair, laid the blue one beside it, then went back to close the door. She sat on the side of the lower bunk and bent forward, covering her face with both hands. After several minutes, she laid on her bunk, staring up at the aluminum coils supporting her sister. She inhaled and exhaled forcefully twice, garnering no response. She cleared her throat loudly with the same result. Finally, she raised her right leg to kick the coils. Kellyanne sat up, punching her mattress with both fists.

"What is your problem, Nellyanne?" she growled.

"Kellyanne, we need to talk about this…"

"That won't be necessary."

"Oh, come on, girl! Are we going to pretend tonight never happened?"

"If it's all the same to you, I'd rather do just that!"

"Well, it's not ok with me! I don't want you to draw the wrong conclusion based on what you saw… To think I'm some kind of—"

"Slut? A little late for that, I'm afraid."

"I was going to say 'whore,' but… same difference, I guess…"

Momentary silence.

"Well, I am neither," Nellyanne continued. "What you saw was a relationship that developed between me and Daddy over time."

"A relationship? You were fucking him, as I recall!!"

More silence. Nellyanne released a long sigh.

"Yes, I was, if you wanna put it bluntly." She paused, trying to find a way to put things into perspective. "But it didn't start out that way…" She sat up, defiantly, on her elbows. "You know, none of this would've happened if not for you!"

Kellyanne snapped to the side of her bunk. She leaned over it with raised eyebrows.   "Excuse me?"

"Yes, you heard me right! Had you not been such a glutton for affection, it never would've come to this!"

"Glutton for what? Affection?"

"Absolutely! Being the first one out of the room every morning. Running through the master bedroom to the bathroom as Daddy was shaving. I got there just in time to see you jump, as he held his razor in one hand, picking you up with the other. The two of you laughing hysterically. All of the time you spent together—weekends included. Playing peek-a-boo at the breakfast table. It was sickening!"

"He *is* my father!"

"Do you hear yourself? OUR father, Kellyanne!"

Kellyanne fell silent… "Why didn't you say something?" she said, now with a softer tone of voice. "Assert yourself? I'm sure he—"

"When did I ever have the chance?" snapped Nellyanne. "There was never a breath of fresh air between the two of you!"

More silence.

"To be honest, I think I understand," said Kellyanne. "You must've felt terribly alone, Nellyanne…"

"I did," said Nellyanne in a lower voice. "And desperate… I had to do something… Anything to turn the tide in my favor…"

Kellyanne propped her head up on her right elbow. "What did you do?" she said. "What could possibly have led to what I saw tonight?"

"It started when Mommy decided to give you the first visit. That night, I lulled you to sleep and took your place."

"Nellyanne!"

"I know, I know… But being you that night made me feel special. For once, *I* was the favorite."

"So what difference did it make?" said Kellyanne. "How did Daddy treat you, thinking you were me?"

"He brought butter brickle ice cream…"

"Damnit, Nellyanne! I would've loved that! I hate to be selfish, but—"

"Then he tricked me into giving him a blowjob!"

Several moments of silence. Kellyanne fell back onto her bunk.

"It evolved from there to actual intercourse when he deemed I was old enough," Nellyanne spoke finally.

"Goodness!" said Kellyanne. "I remember the way it looked! Didn't that hurt? You know, the first time?"

"Not so much, really," she admitted. "Daddy's a handful, but he was gentle… Patient. He took all the time I needed. As time went on, I grew to enjoy it… very much, actually."

More silence.

After more reflection, Kellyanne spoke solemnly, "So, in an effort to betray me, you actually kept me from being raped by my own father?"

"I suppose that's one way to look at it," said Nellyanne softly.

More silence.

"Nellyanne?"

"Yes, Kellyanne."

"Thank you…"

Kellyanne lowered her right hand from the bunk. Nellyanne reached to take it gently with both hands. They let go after several minutes, turned over, and went to sleep.

CHAPTER

SEVEN

The twins woke up the next morning in silence. When Kellyanne came down the ladder, Nellyanne held her waist. They took a moment to look into each other's eyes. They embraced. It was a new day. They both knew it.

They then turned to help each other make the beds. After showering, they dressed—each deliberately choosing a different outfit—looked at the ribbons on the desk, turned and walked arm in arm out of the bedroom.

Mommy had not cooked breakfast. When the door opened and the girls emerged, she and Daddy sat open-mouthed at the dining room table. The newly emancipated sisters spoke a simultaneous "Good morning" and entered the concave kitchen. Unfazed by the change in tradition, Nellyanne took a box of Trix from the center island and grabbed two bowls from the cabinet. Kellyanne retrieved two spoons from the drawer, two glasses from the dishrack, a bottle of orange juice from the refrigerator, and two napkins from the spool by the sink. They put everything on the breakfast nook table and sat down.

Nobody said a word until the girls were finished.

Mommy looked at Daddy, who looked back at her and spoke first, "What? No hug this morning?." He folded his arms, sat back in his seat and waited.

The girls looked at each other, stood, and approached the dining room table. Nellyanne went to hug Mommy, while Kellyanne embraced Daddy. The two then turned to each hug the other parent. They shuffled to gather coats and backpacks from the hall closet, said goodbye, and walked out the front door enroute to school. Mommy and Daddy looked at each other and shook their heads.

After getting off the bus, the remaining blocks home were slow and informative—for Kellyanne.

"So these are *Corny Sutra* positions?" she said, walking backwards for the seminar.

"It's *Kama Sutra*, and you bet!" said Nellyanne. "Some of them are called *postures*, and there's a whole slew of 'em: the posture of the moon, tree with fruit, balance, the swing, the bamboo… You wouldn't believe all the different angles, ways to have sex, Kellyanne," she said, beginning to blush quite noticeably.

"Wow! I want to know them all, Nellyanne," said the flabbergasted look-a-like. "This'll be helpful someday… That is, when and if I ever actually get to have sex…"

"You mean you're still a virgin?" said Nellyanne, coming to a halt, mid-stride. "What about that Idaho boy you were nuts about… Tommy Borders?"

"Yeah, we tried, but let's just say things didn't quite go as planned," said Kellyanne, looking off to her right, momentarily.

"Why? Did it hurt so bad you couldn't go through with it?" said Nellyanne.

"Not exactly," said Kellyanne, gritting her teeth. "He exploded like a volcano before he could even get it in!"

"Really? What did you do?"

"Didn't know what to do. I got up and ran like a bat out of hell!"

They both laughed hysterically as they hugged each other on the sidewalk. After a moment, Nellyanne pulled away and cupped Kellyanne's cheeks.

"You'll have your chance one day, dear," she said. "It'll be awkward at first—painful and uncomfortable—but once you get the hang of it, you'll find it quite enjoyable." Her face turned solemn after a minute; a once tender, reassuring posture was now intense.

"What is wrong with us, Kellyanne?" she said. "We are *twin sisters*. Blood of blood. Flesh of flesh. We're supposed to be super close—to love each other. To be so close nobody can come between us."

Kellyanne's eyes watered. She raised her hands to cover those of her sister. "Why don't we fix that, Nellyanne," she said. "From now on, it's you and me against the world. Nothing, or no one will ever come between us… Ever! How's that sound to you?"

"That's what I truly want. It's what we both need, girl…" She firmly shook her sister's head. "I love you, Kellyanne!"

"I love you too, Nellyanne!! I really do!"

They came together and embraced for several minutes, sobbing uncontrollably.

EIGHT

A hefty right shoulder thrust opened the stubborn, weather-beaten front door. Two steps later, a groan, and a double push closed it. The loud click of a deadbolt. Six spry steps paced the narrow hallway to the guestroom door. A familiar squeal announced entry to a dark and empty room. The door whined shut. Slower footsteps walked the remaining distance to the master bedroom. Two voices mumbled unintelligibly for several minutes. And then there was silence.

Across the hall, the twins exhaled.

"Good night, Nellyanne," the voice whispered from the top bunk.

"Good night, Kellyanne," came the response from below.

They both rolled over and went to sleep.

In the morning, the twins walked out of the bedroom ready for school. Nellyanne was wearing a pink blouse, maroon skirt, white bobbysocks, and burgundy patent leather shoes. Kellyanne wore a navy-blue jean jumpsuit with blue and white Adidas. Mommy sat alone at the dining room table, bending over, with her right arm around her waist. She sat up gingerly when the girls surfaced.

"Nellyanne, you didn't say goodnight to your father last night..." she spoke in the direction of both girls.

Nellyanne stopped to look at her mother as Kellyanne continued on to the kitchen.

"Sorry, Mommy…I fell asleep," she said, shrugging her shoulders.

"Asleep?" Marianne said, holding her stomach as she turned the chair. "How could you, knowing how much it means to him?"

"I know, Mommy," she said. "It's just that—"

"We both have exams today, Mommy," Kellyanne interjected while gathering the bowls. "Took half the night to drill each other until we felt prepared, you know?" She picked up a box of cereal and smiled on the way to the breakfast table.

Mommy looked away and sighed. "Well, that's as good a reason as any, I guess. You girls are juniors now, and you'll need to apply for scholarships soon." She looked back at them. "Suppose you're both getting too old for that sort of thing, anyway, aren't you?"

"Yes ma'am." They spoke in unison as they got on with their new morning routine.

CHAPTER

NINE

The next night's footsteps were slow and staggered. The guestroom was once again dark and empty. This time, the whining door slammed shut, as the steps shuffled haphazardly to the girls' bedroom door and stopped. A shaky hand turned the knob slightly, then released it. The crumbling of a brown paper bag. The loud crash of a bottle shattering against the kitchen wall.

A dining room chair being pulled back from the table. The thud of sitting down. The slow, tentative whine of the master bedroom door. Soft, stockinged feet moved quickly to the table. The sliding of a second chair. A moment of quiet reassurance. The loud, tearful groan of a broken man…

Two nervous souls sat side by side, holding hands tightly on the bottom bunk. Their eyes met in silent celebration of the end of an era. They hugged and climbed into their respective beds.

"Nothing," said Nellyanne.

"Or no one," said Kellyanne.

"Will ever come between us." They finished the slogan together before drifting off to sleep…

The next day began with an empty dining room. There was whispering in the master bedroom. Nellyanne and Kellyanne ate breakfast alone, stood, gathered their belongings and left for school. Neither spoke the entire way, eyes fixed straight ahead on the fourth seat of the desolate bus. The morning air on the way to the stop was crisp and clean—refreshing, as the world seemed to embrace their newfound sense of unshakeable sisterhood. At day's end, after deboarding, the walk home was much livelier. They needed a plan of action moving forward.

"What are we going to say to Mommy and Daddy?" said Kellyanne, slowing to a standstill just three blocks into the journey; hands on hips. "Daddy's going to want answers…"

"I can handle him," said Nellyanne, waving her left hand at her sister. "He tends to growl initially, but then go with the flow… I'm more concerned about Mommy. She doesn't look good. Did you see her yesterday?" she said, placing her left hand on Kellyanne's right shoulder.

"Yes, I did," said Kellyanne. "I'm worried too. This whole thing has got to be extremely difficult for her." She paused for a moment before looking at Nellyanne with narrowed eyes.

"Are you sure this is the best way to put an end to things?" she said. "You know, forcing Daddy to kick it cold turkey and all?"

"I don't see any other way," said Nellyanne, shaking her head.

"But won't that be awkward for you too?" said Kellyanne, remembering her sister's reference to a "relationship" with Daddy.

"Not really," Nellyanne said, looking down. "In the beginning, it was all so fresh and new… Exciting. But after I got my first period, it started to really hit me. Something is terribly wrong here! This is not the way things are supposed to be. This is my father, for Christ's sake!" She looked up and into the concerned eyes of Kellyanne. "I've wanted to end it for quite some time now. Just never had the courage until you caught us and forced the issue…"

"I can't even imagine," said Kellyanne. "I mean, who would think the first boyfriend they'd ever have to break up with would be their father?"

"Sounds so much worse when I hear you say it," said Nellyanne. "But it's over… Time to branch out and test the waters for boys my age."

"Now that's a mission we can embark on together," Kellyanne said with a little shimmy.

"I'm surprised it's taken you so long," Nellyanne said, looking down at Kellyanne's pleated green and yellow skirt.

"You've still got that Ferrari parked in neutral?"

"Yes ma'am," said Kellyanne, forming an imaginary chastity belt around her waist. "Waiting for the one I deem worthy enough to drive it!"

"Well, don't wait too long, sis. It'll develop rust, you know…"

"Oh, don't you worry," said Kellyanne, waving her index finger. "I keep it waxed and buffed."

"Yeah… I know."

"You do? How?"

"You toss and turn at night, Kellyanne," she said, flashing a wry smile. "Especially after I've had a visit on your behalf with Daddy. Once you think I'm asleep, I can hear the covers shuffling. You can muffle an orgasm, but the breathing afterward gives you away. I know that sound, believe me."

Kellyanne blushed bright pink. She placed both hands on her hips. "Well," she said, looking up at the sky. "If you're gonna get busted, it may as well be by your identical twin…"

They screamed with laughter and turned to keep walking.

CHAPTER

TEN

Marianne proofread the three-page letter once more before folding it neatly and placing it in an envelope. She licked the seal and walked slowly toward the grandfather clock. It was Nellyanne's turn to wipe the glass. Turning the corner at the end of the dining room table, a searing pain struck her chest and abdomen. She slammed the hand with the envelope on the table to break her fall, landing on both knees. Her left arm stiffened. She could hardly breathe. She looked to the digital phone on the center island miles away…

"Marianne!"

When she opened her eyes, Bucky was on his knees at her side. Unable to speak, Marianne's eyes rotated to the center island, then back at him. He looked up, stood, and ran to the phone.

"Hello? Yes, I need an ambulance at 4200 East Franklin Lane. My wife is in trouble. She's on the dining room floor. She can't speak. She can't move. Please hurry!"

When he returned, she lay there, face contorted but eyes still open. She managed to slowly raise her right hand. Bucky held it with both hands, trembling. He could tell she was trying to smile.

"Stay with me, honey," he pleaded. "Help is on the way. I love you, Marianne… I love you so much!"

The all too familiar wavering sound of a siren pierced the quiet air, coming to a halt not far from the girls. Kellyanne broke into a lively sprint for the final block, stopped at the street corner, and raised both hands to her mouth.

"Kellyanne! What is it?" said Nellyanne, speeding up her own pace. "What's wrong?"

Without answering, Kellyanne began to run. Nellyanne followed suit, sensing trouble.

The white Ford with blue and orange stripes had arrived at the destination. Its back doors remained open. The twins raced up the winding path to the porch steps. Mommy laid on a portable litter, with paramedics working frantically to her right and left, with an oxygen mask over her nose and mouth. Daddy stood off to the right, hands to mouth, tears streaming down both cheeks. He turned his head toward the girls as they entered.

"She was on the floor when I got here," he said with bated breath. "Looked like she was trying to get to the phone. We're on the way to the hospital. I'm gonna walk beside your mother to the ambulance. You girls put your things away. You can ride with me in the cab…"

They removed their backpacks and headed past the cot to the bedroom, with Kellyanne in front. Mommy grabbed Nellyanne's right hand tightly as she passed. Nellyanne stopped to look down at her. Mommy's eyes rolled to the corner of the dining room table, then back to Nellyanne. Nellyanne glanced across the room, located the envelope, looked back at her mom, and nodded. Mommy let go as the medics whisked her away.

CHAPTER
ELEVEN

The pristine waiting room was dry, unwelcoming. The firm bolted chairs made Nellyanne feel as if she wasn't supposed to be there long. Daddy had been talking to the doctor in another area for what seemed like hours, while the twins sat silent with fingers clasped in their laps. He returned to stand in front of them with slumped shoulders.

"It doesn't look good," he said slowly. "The cancer has spread. They've sedated and stabilized her. Done all they could. You can go in—preferably one at a time—and say your goodbyes."

Nellyanne looked at her sister. "Why don't you go ahead, Kellyanne," she said.

Kellyanne stood, took a deep breath, and wiped a tear from the corner of her right eye.

"I'll show you the room, dear." Daddy took her by the left hand, as they walked away.

Nellyanne pressed her back against the chair with glazed eyes. She began to reflect on events that culminated in this sudden, yet inevitable moment: the look on Mommy's face after inserting the last bobby pin into her hair for that first ribbon; the way she lifted Nellyanne high in the air and spun her around when she'd memorized her ABC's; the way she'd scratch her head in agony when attempting to help both girls with algebra, geometry, and trigonometry; her stern demeanor—especially toward Kellyanne—when teaching them what women "are supposed to do…" The dark, constant mental image of Mommy standing at the guestroom door, shaking her head with hands on hips, as Nellyanne had sex with Daddy…

She reached into her blouse to retrieve the white envelope…

"My Dearest Nellyanne,

"Although I would've loved to have seen you girls grow up, find mates and have your own families, play with my grandchildren and even great grandchildren, I accept Heaven's sentencing of a shortened life as karma for the wrong I've done. My failures as a wife pale in comparison to those as a mother. I pray you and your sister will someday find it in your hearts to forgive me.

Jerome Summers is not your father. His brother, Matthew, was a police officer, killed in the line of duty during a drug raid. He died shortly after we became pregnant—with twins, and before we could marry. Jerome proposed to assume responsibility out of loyalty to his brother. The fact that I never knew my father and was deathly afraid of being alone greatly influenced my decision to accept. It was my first mistake. Together, we were never able to achieve the level of intimacy I shared with Matthew. As a result, I lived for years with the expectation he would eventually leave me."

Nellyanne stopped reading when she noticed a Puerto Rican family of five enter the waiting room in tears. When the youngest of the children, a little boy with a crew cut, white khaki pants, and a black polo shirt looked her way—seemingly for an explanation—she looked down and listened. Her Spanish was shaky, but apparently, the mother, a long-haired, woman with smooth, caramel skin, clutching a gray burlap coat over a red sundress was trying to explain what had happened to their father. Nellyanne felt better, somehow, knowing she was not alone, and beginning to understand her mother's plight. She continued reading:

> *"I was always harder on Kellyanne because I realized she thrived within an atmosphere of discipline. She has her father's determination and her mother's tendency to use detachment to avoid pain. You, on the other hand, have always been more rational, able to find answers to complex questions more easily. You've unfortunately inherited my dysfunctional need for emotional support at all costs. I want you to help Kellyanne navigate her way through difficult situations, but step back and let her find her way when the time comes. And in your search for love, be careful not to let wrong choices lead you astray! Never lose sight of who you are.*
>
> *"It is becoming increasingly difficult to hold this pen, so I will end by saying this: Maintain the bond you have forged with your sister. I will be watching the two of you from afar soon, and I want to be able to smile when I do. You are both extraordinary young women. I loved you more than you will ever know…*
>
> *Mommy"*

Nellyanne watched the tears fall on the last portion of the letter. She straightened her back, folded it, placed it neatly back into the envelope, into her blouse, and patted it twice.

"Thank you, Mommy," she whispered, as she gathered herself for her turn to say goodbye.

CHAPTER

TWELVE

Fresh out of high school, the Summers twins were elated to receive letters of acceptance from University Hill! The admissions board was impressed, not only with their academic achievements while living within a social demographic where many students faltered, but also with the thought of having identical and indistinguishable twins on the student body roster. On the first day of registration, the girls signed up to major in *education*, with aspirations to teach at the college level someday. Nellyanne double majored in *educational counseling*. Kellyanne minored in *civil service*—Nellyanne in *guerilla warfare*. She figured anyone who could survive a childhood like hers must have latent warrior instincts.

Halfway through sophomore year, Kellyanne finally lost her virginity to Jonathan 'Sonny-Boy' Pearson, star quarterback of the orange men's varsity football team. Nellyanne took full advantage of the smorgasbord of young freshmen who were anxious to benefit from her sexual prowess and vast experience. Both finished at the top of the class, with prominent recognition on the dean's list.

Daddy attended the graduation in a pinstriped Brooks Brothers suit. He smiled broadly and clapped loudly as they walked across the stage. Wrinkles lined his forehead and the dry skin beneath his cheekbones that grew deeper with changes in facial expressions. He now walked with a cane and sat sooner than the jubilant crowd around him. Mommy's life insurance policy gave him the freedom to pay off the house. But life as he knew it had taken its toll. He would be dead in a year.

After graduation, the recession made finding jobs in their chosen fields of study extremely difficult. Nellyanne suggested they explore employment opportunities abroad and return when conditions improve. Kellyanne wanted to become a cop. That way, she would be doing something commiserate with her minor. Nellyanne acquiesced to keep them together. They entered Flushing Police Academy in the fall.

Kellyanne excelled, achieving honors at every phase of the program. She was a natural—a favorite of the commandant's office. But Nellyanne struggled. She'd signed up to be a cop—not a robot, barking "Yes sir!" and "No sir!" to every Tom, Dick, and Harry passing by with rank. She failed to graduate—deemed "*psychologically unfit for police duty*".

"So what'll we do now, sis?" Nellyanne spoke, as they shared a tub of butter brickle in the atrium.

"What do you mean?"

"Well, we're not going to be sister cops. That door's been shut…"

"Maybe for you…"

"Don't tell me you're actually going to go through with this! How could you do that?"

"Nellyanne, this whole experience has changed me. I've discovered a part of myself I didn't know existed. I really want to be a police officer!"

"But what about us? What will become of the team? Our plans?"

"You are my sister. I love you. What I do for a living will not change that. Nothing or no one will ever come between us, right?"

Nellyanne smirked. "What about the house?" she said. "Wanna sell it and move to Manhattan?"

"I've got my eye on a nice little Brownstone apartment there already. Closer to the police department. You can keep it. Even rent it out if you want."

"I don't like the idea of us no longer living together, Kellyanne."

"But don't you think it's time? We'll be working in different fields, different hours, dating, later marrying and starting our own families. I mean sooner or later this was bound to happen, right?"

She raised the spoon in her right hand to offer Nellyanne another scoop. Nellyanne grabbed her wrist and gently lowered the peace offering back into the tub. She stood with hands on hips.

"You finish it. Think I've had enough for one day…" She took three steps backward. "Have a nice graduation and life afterward, Kellyanne. You've earned it. Did this one on your own. Got this whole thing figured out. Certainly don't need me anymore…"

"Nellyanne, that's not true! Nellyanne… Sis!"

Her words echoed across the recreational area as loud, disgruntled footsteps took her sister farther and farther away…

"Is the line ready?" A clear, crisp voice from the corner speaker paused as the steel-toed monitor made his way down the Formica path to the last shooter. He turned to give a thumbs-up to an unseen observer.

"The line *is* ready…FIRE!"

Shots reverberated along the firing line. The tinkling of empty fifteen-round magazine cartridges as they hit the floor was evident despite the blizzard of gunfire. Charging of fresh cartridges preceded more shots until the sixty-second buzzer sounded.

"CEASE FIRE! CEASE FIRE!"

A few late shots went off before the line was silent.

Kellyanne holstered her glock-19, lowered her Walker digital muffs, and pressed the retrieval button to summon her target. She watched intently, as it traveled the long transport wire. When it arrived, she took it down and smiled. Twenty-eight of thirty true hits. Twenty-six of them struck center mass! Overcome with admiration, she didn't notice the man approaching to her right.

"Impressive!" he said, flashing a set of pearly white teeth.

Kellyanne removed her eyewear and stretched to look into the eyes of what appeared to be a Wakandan Warrior. He was tall, built like a body builder/aerobics instructor, with a short wavy black semi-perm, her father's hazel eyes, neatly trimmed eyebrows, a thin mustache that ended precisely at each corner of the mouth, and smooth ebony skin. He was absolutely gorgeous! She hadn't been stricken in this way since Tommy Borders…

"Thank you," she said, holding the target at shoulder level for the purpose of joint admiration. "Took a minute to get used to, but I think it turned out ok."

"Yeah, the sights are tricky, and the grip can be challenging, but it's a great piece once you get used to it," he said, pointing to the shots wide of center mass. "I prefer the MOS, but I guess we have to take what they give us…"

"I've heard similar comments," she said, admiring his square shoulders and v-neck body shirt. "This your final qualifier?"

"Yep," he said, still smiling. "It's on to the precinct from here."

"Me too. Where are they sending you?"

"The thirteenth."

"Really? Me too." She spoke, trying to hide her enthusiasm. She extended her right hand. "I'm Kellyanne… Kellyanne Summers."

"Bernard Williams," he said, taking her hand firmly, eyes pausing at her chest before shaking it. "Pleased to meet you, Kellyanne."

"Pleased to meet you, Bernard," she said, pretending not to notice his involuntary slip in social etiquette. She sat her target down, while realizing he didn't have his. "How'd you do, by the way?"

"I did ok," he said, quickly glancing at his watch. "Coming up on 9 o'clock. We should be heading for the precinct. I hear Captain Grant is a stickler for punctuality. Let me get my range bag."

He turned to walk back to his station. Kellyanne grabbed her bag and followed him. His hips and glutes were poetry in motion. She stopped to watch them become even more pronounced with the admiration of one beholding a freshly baked Christmas turkey as he gathered his belongings. Her eyes shifted momentarily to the target he left on the station pedestal. Her mouth opened when she saw the results. Thirty out of thirty true hits. Twenty-nine center mass…One forehead center!! She looked away as he straightened up, throwing the bag over his right shoulder.

"Hey, there's a Starbucks on the way," he said. "We've got a little time. Can I buy you a cup of coffee?"

"Actually, that sounds great!" she said. "I could really go for a cappuccino with a honey twist right about now. I'll follow you there."

"You got it," he said as they left the building.

CHAPTER

FOURTEEN

On a foggy September day, newscasts warned of bumper-to-bumper traffic on Madison Avenue northbound, from Madison Square to Harlem River Drive. Bright yellow tape with large block letters formed a fifteen-foot enclosure around the entrance of Dolce and Gabbana. Charlie Rosencrantz, an NYPD medical examiner assigned to Manhattan's thirteenth precinct, knelt on one knee beside the victim. She was a young, Caucasian redhead, average height, physically fit. Late teens/early twenties, wearing a blood-soaked blue and white cheerleader outfit from Columbia University. Early holiday shoppers surrounded the perimeter along the sidewalk, restrained by a barricade of police officers. From the street, stranded travelers in cars, buses, and taxis, pointed and gazed at the spectacle.

Detective Kellyanne Summers entered the area, flanked by Deputies Ricky Fresno to her right and Bobby Caine to her left.

"What've we got here, Charlie?" she said with hands on hips.

Charlie sprang to his feet, pushed his black-rimmed glasses up the bridge of his narrow nose, cleared his throat and smiled.

"Good morning, Detective Summers," he said. "Looks like a GSW to the chest. Judging by entry and exit wounds, a high-powered rifle, fired from a distance."

"How long has she been here?" she said, walking the length of the body.

"Body temperature and lividity suggest she's been dead six to ten hours. But the absence of blood spatter indicates she was shot elsewhere and moved here."

"Any idea of the bullet's caliber?"

"Exit wound suggests a rather large caliber. I'll need to measure and run some tests back at the lab."

"Wouldn't be Manhattan without a murder in September, would it?"

Summers, Fresno, and Caine shifted abruptly.

He was tall and slender, with curly blonde hair, aquamarine eyes, wearing a black, pinstriped Botany 500 suit, matching tie and white silk shirt.

"Sir, this is a crime scene," said Fresno, firmly placing his left hand on the man's chest.

"We're going to have to ask you to leave," said Caine.

"You'll need to remain outside the perimeter," Summers said, reaching for his left arm.

"Who let him in here? Jamie…"

The young cadet turned from the boundary line to acknowledge her aggravated superior. "He has authorization, ma'am."

The stranger straightened his tie. pulled his onyx cufflinks to the wrists and extended his right hand. "Forgive my manners. I'm Peter… Peter Castellano… Captain Grant sent me."

Fresno lowered his arm. Summers returned hands to hips.

Leaving his hand extended, Peter couldn't help but notice her beauty: long, wavy black hair, the widow's peak, emerald-green eyes, small, tapered nose, tanned complexion, and strong jaw line.

"Captain Grant?" she said. "Why would he—"

"I'm your new partner…"

Summers squinted, pursed her lips, then walked past him to address the two open-mouthed deputies.

"Canvas the area," she said. "See if anyone saw or heard anything in the last twenty-four hours. And check for traffic cams. Maybe we'll get lucky with some footage of what the hell happened here."

She turned toward the white patrol car with blue horizontal stripes parked curbside of the perimeter. Peter looked at his abandoned hand, shrugged his shoulders and lowered it. He reached for his cell phone.

"Where're you headed, ma'am?" Caine said.

"Back to the precinct!" she said, with a back-handed wave in stride.

Charlie shook his head, covered the victim with a dark blue leather tarp, and called for transport.

FIFTEEN

Officers Summers and Williams approached the Dutch Colonial residence brandishing weapons shoulder high, arms fully extended. The warm, subtropical air carried the vinegary scent of fentanyl past the open plate glass window, several feet into the front yard. Williams reached the door, knocked three times, and turned his back to rest against the wall to the left.

"NYPD! OPEN THE DOOR NOW," he exclaimed, motioning to Summers, who stood at the ready.

A frantic movement of furniture ensued. The sound of quick footsteps, an opening interior door that immediately slammed shut. Williams swung around, took two steps backward, fired twice at the lock and turned the knob.

"NYPD!" he announced once inside. Summers hustled to back him up.

Repeater shots shattered the living room window and spread around the room from within. Summers hit the ground, then crawled toward the door. When the firing stopped, she crouched and entered. Two men lay slumped over a long, grey sofa, two lay sprawled behind the prep table. Two others lay motionless on the living room floor. One of them was Officer Williams. The others looked to be *Silenciosos*.

Kellyanne moved to clear the room, then returned to her fallen partner.

"Attention all units! Officer Kellyanne Summers, reporting an eleven-thirty-one at 5516 Manchester Road. Shots fired. Officer down. Multiple casualties. Need immediate assistance!" She put the radio down and began administering CPR. "Call for backup, Bernie!" she screamed between chest pumps. "We should call for fucking backup! After seven years… you'd think… just maybe… I might be right!"

But Bernie was unresponsive. His head, arms, and legs were riddled with bullets. Both of his ears were missing.

In the distance, Kellyanne heard the garage door opening slowly. With glock in hand, she felt her body stand, and in a zombie-like state, turned to walk out the front door. On the porch, she saw the shiny, slow-moving hood of a black El Camino Real.

"Hola, Chica!" The voices chimed in unison as shots erupted from the front and back passenger windows.

Zing after zing passed to the right, left and above her, spraying the timber walls and flared eaves overhead. But Kellyanne stood tall, returning fire. Seven shots hit home. The car crashed into a nearby fire hydrant, sending water streaming in all directions. With her weapon still trained on the target, she approached the vehicle. When she arrived, the driver and three passengers lay slumped in their respective seats.

"Vaya con Dios, gentlemen," she murmured before holstering the glock.

She stood, stoic, with glazed eyes, for a moment before shifting to make the journey back to him. To Bernie—her partner—her friend—her lover and confidant—her world. She dropped to her knees at his side, closed his eyelids, laid her head on his chest, and gave herself permission to unleash a reservoir of tears. She wrapped her right arm around his waist, vowing to hold him until reinforcements arrived.

SIXTEEN

Captain Ulysses Arthur Grant was a person Kellyanne admired. An ex-army sniper, he'd spent thirty-five years on the force—including five in narcotics, three undercover, and two in domestic terrorism—before being promoted from lieutenant to captain with minimal time in grade. When the promotion board balked at offering a detective slot to the first woman in department history, he fought to get them to consider only her qualifications. He groomed her and helped her navigate the waters of gender-inequality prevalent at the time. It was he who paired her up with Bernie years ago.

Celeste, his wife of thirty years, was an adjunct professor at Weill Cornell Medical College, where both daughters, Melanie and Christine, graduated with honors. Grant was a fair man who believed in justice. He was also the only person Summers would allow to call her "Kelly". That honor she'd reserved for her deceased father.

Daddy believed a name like Kellyanne sounded more like a signature than a name. "Too formal," he would say. "No love in it, dear." It seemed he had a valid point. Teachers at school and Mommy only addressed her as "Kellyanne," usually when demanding she do something. Always for purpose—never with genuine affection. But when he was tickling her during television commercials, pretending to enjoy the dry cakes she made with her Easy-Bake Oven, or carrying her on his shoulders while birdwatching in the backyard, she was always—always "Kelly". When he died, Kellyanne buried that memory with him. That is, until she met Captain Grant...

Standing in stark contrast to its meager inception in 1845, the newly renovated station house now bustled like Grand Central. Double-pedestal wooden desks with cherry finishes sat on a polished, laminated wood floor in two rows on both sides of the spacious, rectangular administrative area. They were evenly spaced, separated by an eighteen-inch center aisle. The soft, lemony scent of Bona Industrial floor cleaner lingered in the air. Some deputies sat fielding complaints ranging from missing persons to domestic violence. Others answered phones and dispatched uniforms.

Detective Summers walked past Deputy Chung, who waited patiently for an elderly woman with thick, round glasses to look through photos of prior offenders. She greeted him with an upward head nod. He smiled and returned the gesture.

"Detective Summers. A word?"

Captain Grant stood at his office door. He'd loosened his tie and two buttons at the collar.

Summers lowered her eyes as she walked toward him. He stepped aside, closed the door behind her, and drew the window shades. She sat on the burgundy sofa against a long, white wall across from his large mahogany desk. He walked behind it, sat down and sighed. Leaning forward, he clasped his fingers, placed both forearms on the glass-top surface and looked at her.

"Got a call from the field," he said. "Apparently, you're not happy with me..."

"Sir, I don't need a partner."

"Manpower doc says I have to give you one... Kelly, we've been through this."

"I have the highest closure rate in the thirteenth. I just don't see why—"

"It's regulation, Detective. Can't get around this one."

She took a deep breath, looked to the ceiling, back at Grant, and exhaled.

"Look, we've all experienced loss, Kelly," he said. "Comrades, partners, family, but we move on. We keep going."

"That's not it, sir..."

"He's a great guy. He's—"

"Arrogant!" She sat upright and expanded her chest. "He shows up at the crime scene, and the first thing he says is—"

"I told him to be himself," Grant asserted. "Don't want him walking on eggshells around you… Try to look past the brash exterior, Kelly. He's extremely capable. Highest closure rate in the nineteenth."

"Then why is he here?" she said, tilting her head forward. "What was the problem back at the nineteenth?"

Grant sat back in his oversized black leather chair. "That's a topic the two of you can broach sometime later… Consider it part of the process. Getting to know each other."

"What about Fresno and Caine?"

"They're sharp guys. I've got plans for both of them."

Summers looked to her right, clasped her fingers in her lap, and twirled her thumbs.

"Give it a chance, Kelly," he said. "Thirty days. If it doesn't work out, I'll send him back quicker than a crow can shit with his ass wide open!"

She felt an involuntary chuckle escape her lips. Their eyes met in solidarity.

"Thirty days?"

"Thirty days."

They stood. Kellyanne walked to his desk. They shook hands. He opened the door.

In the far northwest corner, Peter waited patiently in the seat next to her desk. Summers turned to look back at Captain Grant. He smiled and closed the office door. Peter had removed his coat, neatly placing it over the back of his chair. Two large containers labeled "Starbucks" were situated in plain view. She rolled her seat back and sat down.

"What's this?" she said, tilting her head to read the black, vertical stickers.

"Yours is a double cappuccino with a honey twist."

"Really? How… did you know?"

"Fresno and Caine briefed me."

"And yours?"

"Triple espresso, straight up."

"Too strong for me," she said with a shiver. "After one of those, I'd be wired all day."

"Yes, I know…" Peter straightened his tie. "Hey, I want to apologize for the way I came off back there. Not great at first impressions…"

"Yeah, I gathered that."

"Tend to joke when I'm nervous. Meeting the renowned Detective Summers for the first time… A bit intimidating, you know?"

"Renowned?"

"Oh yeah! You're a legend back at the nineteenth. The men envy you and the women want to be you. They all admire you."

She remembered the talk with Grant. Now was as good a time as any…

"Speaking of the nineteenth," she spoke softly. "What brought about the transfer? That is, if you don't mind me asking."

Peter reached for his cup, lifted the lid, and leaned back.

"Not at all," he said. "I lost my partner, Stephanie, during a drug raid. She went in first. They were waiting."

"Wow! I lost Bernie the same way."

"My condolences. I hear Detective Williams was a good man."

"The best. How long… You and Stephanie, I mean?"

"Seven years. You two?"

"Seven years, three months, and four days."

"I've been where you are. Drew X's on my desk calendar until I couldn't do it anymore. Lost focus. My performance suffered. Captain Richter felt a change would do me good. He spoke with Captain Grant. They thought a move down here would benefit both of us."

"Were you and Stephanie that close?"

"Put it this way. We had reservations for a celebratory dinner after the bust. I—"

"That's pretty benign. Bernie and I always went for drinks afterward. There's this place off—"

"I was going to propose…"

Their eyes met in a frozen silence.

The desk phone rang twice.

"Detective Summers… Hi, Charlie… Ok. We'll be right there." She hung up, pushed back away from the desk and stood. "The M.E. has something for us."

Peter stood and grabbed his coat.

CHAPTER

SEVENTEEN

Charlie stood at the examination table in a white lab coat, wearing horn-rimmed bifocals as he glared into a thick weapons manual. He looked up, removed his glasses and greeted them, this time without a smile.

"Detectives, we have a problem."

He shuffled across the checkerboard floor and placed the book on a white veneer reading desk. He then turned and walked past the body over to a stainless-steel double-basin sink to retrieve a pair of PF nitrile gloves. After inserting fingers and snapping each one loudly at the wrists, Charlie walked to the table, rolled back the tarp and tilted the corpse just enough to reveal the gaping hole in its back.

"In thirty years," he said solemnly, "I've never seen this level of damage inflicted by a single gunshot. I doubt you have either…"

Summers took three steps backward, raising both hands to her mouth.

"Trace results confirm this is the work of a DSR-1, compact-bolt action precision sniper rifle," Charlie said, sensing the need to get on with it. "It's German-made. A very powerful weapon."

"I'm familiar with it," Peter said. "We've worked with countries all over Europe to assess its capabilities in joint counter-terrorism maneuvers."

"What's it doing here?" Summers spoke, lowering her left hand.

"I don't know," said Peter. "But this technology used to be kept under lock and key. Reserved for only elite security forces."

"That's right, Detective Castellano," Charlie said, returning the body to its original position.

As he restored the tarp, Summers lowered her right hand.

"This shooter is a highly trained marksman. Versed in a skill originally reserved for select members of law enforcement. He may be a disgruntled European ex-cohort, a terrorist implant, or—"

"One of us," said Summers, now with hands on hips. "Any idea where she died?"

"Not sure, but I did find this stamp just below the palm of her left hand." Charlie adjusted the tarp just enough to reveal it.

"Paris Blues," said Summers. "Looks like she'd been out sometime before she died. Can't say that I recognize the name, though…"

"No, I've heard of this place," said Peter. "It's a ritzy jazz club in lower East Harlem."

"Do we know who she is, Charlie?" said Summers.

"Not yet," he said. "I ran dentals, prints, and trace up to forensics. They're busy, though. Could take a while."

"Good work, Charlie." She turned to Peter. "We need to get back. Fresno and Caine may have something by now."

Back at the main house, Summers and Castellano returned to her desk. As they sat, she whisked a loose strand of hair behind her left ear. Peter smiled and reached for his espresso. Kellyanne looked at him, tapped her fingers on the desk, and reached for her cappuccino.

"East Harlem," he spoke. "That's the twenty-third. I know a guy up there—Jimmy Breslin. We grew up together in Champlain. Maybe he knows something."

"Great idea," said Summers, raising the cup to her lips. "We can use all the help we can get on this one, Detective."

"You can call me Peter, by the way."

"Kellyanne."

"That seems like a mouthful… Can I call you Kelly?"

Her glare was sufficient. Peter blinked and took a sip.

Fresno and Caine walked in the front door; coats flung with fingers over their right shoulders. Kellyanne and Peter stood as they approached.

"What've we got?" she said, hands on hips.

"Still canvasing, but nothing yet," said Caine. "Waiting for traffic cams. Do we know who the victim is?"

"Not yet," she said. "Charlie sent dentals, prints, and trace up to forensics."

"Going on five o'clock," said Fresno. "Probably won't have anything until tomorrow."

"Yeah, Charlie says they're pretty busy," she said, placing her right hand on Fresno's left shoulder.

"You know what? Let's call it a day. Detective Castellano and I will brief the captain, and we'll hit the ground running first thing in the morning."

CHAPTER

EIGHTEEN

Judith Anderson. Twenty years old. Born in Queens. Junior at Columbia University. Sociology major. Dean's list. Head cheerleader of the lions' men's varsity basketball team. Both parents, Frank and Margaret, are resident physicians at Presbyterian Hospital.

After identifying the body, Kellyanne and Peter led the Andersons through central processing to a private, mahogany wood-paneled conference room. After being relieved of their coats, the somber couple were seated at a round, blue and white marble table with four high-back chairs.

Kellyanne centered the omnidirectional microphone between them and sat beside Peter to begin the interview.

"Mr. and Mrs. Anderson, let me begin by saying we're sorry for your loss," she said, taking a moment to make direct eye contact with each one. "Was your daughter having any problems with anyone? Acting differently? Any concerns about her safety? And do you know how often she would go to East Harlem?"

"No problems with anyone that we know of," said Mrs. Anderson. "She seemed fine… Happy. And there is no earthly reason she'd be in that place!" She looked at her husband, who shook his head at the detectives.

"Ma'am?" said Kellyanne.

"I mean, she's always been a rebel of sorts, you know?" Mrs. Anderson leaned forward. "A free spirit. But we didn't raise her to—"

Mr. Anderson touched her left hand.

The detectives looked at each other.

"Did she have any close friends?" said Kellyanne, shifting the focus to Mr. Anderson.

"She was a popular girl, but rather selective in personal relationships," he said. "Only one girl ever came up to the house… Helen Pace."

"Maybe she can help shed some light on the events leading up to this unfortunate incident…"

"It's possible…They seemed inseparable…"

Kellyanne stood. "Is there anything else either of you can tell us that might help find the person who did this?"

Both parents shook their heads while standing.

"Thank you so much for your time. And again, please accept our heartfelt condolences."

"When can we take her home?" said Mrs. Anderson, reaching into her pink, Gucci handbag for a satin seashell handkerchief.

"We're still in the early stages of the investigation," said Kellyanne. "I promise to call as soon as you can do that. You have my word."

Helen Pace arrived later that afternoon. She was a rather tall, buxom platinum blonde with a braided ponytail, long bangs. The words "Heart of a Lion" had been tattooed across the top of her left hand. She blinked often during questioning, twirling a pair of thin-rimmed prescription glasses in her right hand.

"She usually went up there a couple times a month," she said. "Her boyfriend, Jarrod, is the starting point guard for our basketball team. He lives there. Judith was his global economics tutor. Great guy, but she knew her parents would never approve. The two of them always went to this jazz club she raved about—Paris Blues. But she was back by Sunday evening. We were going through some routines on speakerphone when she got an incoming call and had to hang up. We planned to meet for practice the next day. She never showed. I knew then something was terribly wrong. I mean, this is a person who lived to wear that uniform… To be the leader of our squad. She never missed a practice… Wouldn't do that!" She slammed her fist on the table, then looked away.

Kellyanne gently slid the Kleenex box closer to her…

When the interview was over, Caine stood waiting outside the door.

"Cam footage is in. There's something you both need to see."

CHAPTER

NINETEEN

Nellyanne attacked the Canadian rapids with reckless abandon. She screamed with delight as the kayak carved the path she paved through crystal blue water.

It just doesn't get any better than this, she thought, inhaling the cool, fresh air and loving the warmth of the midday sun.

With every stroke of the paddle, she thrashed away anger, frustration, and loneliness. This was where she belonged. Free from traffic jams, pollution, and people. Just her… and the water. Here, she was free!

Her moment of bliss evaporated in an instant, replaced by the horrific realization that she had made a terrible mistake. Somehow, she'd navigated off-course into an unfamiliar area. Worse still, she saw the seventy-five-foot drop-off ahead. The kayak began to obey the vacuum controlling the current. Nellyanne fought to keep from being jettisoned. She gripped the paddle and summoned her resolve.

"Come on, girl," she commanded. "You've got this. Feet firm… Butt solid… Hand spacing and finger placement on the shaft… Flip the blades… Let's go!"

She pulled back and leaned with all her might. Leaning forward, she repeated the movement, time and time again. The river cried out in angry disobedience, fighting the paddle blades with every stroke. Nellyanne felt her arms and upper body begin to tire, as the boat turned completely around, being pulled from behind. Water spilled across her lap and swallowed her feet. Her efforts failed, as the kayak turned once more to face the cliff ahead. Nellyanne closed her eyes to await the inevitable…

Out of nowhere, a massive arm surrounded her torso, dislodging her from the canoe. Nellyanne screamed as the stranger pinned her body to his right side, pressed the red button on a long, wired mechanism, and held her as it pulled them both to the safe, marshy bank. Now breathing heavily, he disconnected the hoist, dragged her further inland, and laid on his back next to her. After several minutes, he stood, walked uphill to his Ford F-150, and returned with a burlap blanket. He smiled and nudged her lightly under the left shoulder. Nellyanne sat up, still shaking, and helped him drape it around her. He stepped back with folded arms and looked at her.

"I… don't know how… to thank you…" she said, noticing for the first time the sheer size of the Good Samaritan.

He stood well over six feet tall, massive broad shoulders, wearing a red and white checkered cotton shirt, blue jeans, a pair of tanned Brogans, and a bright red cap that appeared to cover a bald head. A huge pot belly strained the shirt buttons at his waist. A full, reddish-brown beard made his prominent nose look small. He had beautiful baby blue eyes.

"Pleasure to do it, ma'am," he said, removing his hat, confirming his baldness. "Just glad I happened to be passing by."

"As am I," she said, managing a smile as she stood. "I'm Nellyanne, by the way," she said, extending her right hand, while clutching the blanket at the neck with her left. "Nellyanne Summers…"

"Richard," he said, taking her hand. "Richard Glasgow. You can call me Ricky. You from around here?"

"No. I'm from New York… The Bronx. I come out here once a year on vacation. Are you from Canada?"

"Pennsylvania," he said with a headshake. "I come out here to hunt from time to time… What happened out there?"

"I don't know," she said, turning to look back at the river. "Made a right when I should've gone left, I guess. Lost track of where I was on the water. It's not like me to do something like that…"

"We all make mistakes, Nellyanne," he said. "Important thing is, you're ok."

"I'll drink to that," she said, beginning to warm under the blanket. "Speaking of drinks… Can I offer you a cup of coffee? I mean, it's the least I can do…"

"Sure… I think I'd like that."

"Great! I rent a cabin right up the road. Follow me there?"

"Sounds like a plan."

Back at the cabin, Richard proved to be very pleasant company. They talked for hours over several cups of coffee. He was a lumberjack with a somewhat blemished past. His father was a drug addict, his mother an alcoholic. He ran away from home at the age of sixteen, living on the streets of Philadelphia for years before learning the tree cutting trade to make an honest living. He'd never been married and was not currently attached. By nightfall, Nellyanne bid him goodnight, thanked him again, and went to bed.

Bright and early the next morning, Richard arrived with an invitation to breakfast. Reluctantly, Nellyanne accepted. They had pancakes, eggs, hashbrowns, and coffee. They talked until Nellyanne saw the way he was looking at her.

"Look, Richard," she said, touching his left hand. "Ricky… I don't want to be rude. You're a very nice person, but I'm afraid this can never be more than a friendship at best. I truly appreciate all you've done for me, but—"

"I know, Nellyanne," he said, gently patting her extended hand. "You're way out of my league."

"It's not that. I'm just not—"

"It's true," he interjected. "And I'm okay with that." He sat his right elbow on the table and began to stroke his beard. "Since we're being transparent, you should know the truth," he said, looking down at the table. "I saw you a couple years ago, and thought you were the most beautiful woman I'd ever seen. I followed you to the cabin and talked to the owner, Mr. Jefferson, when you left. He told me when you'd be back, and I wait for you every year."

Nellyanne sat back in her chair.

"Don't get me wrong, Nellyanne," he continued. "I'm not a pervert. I'm not a stalker. I just…" He raised his right index finger. "…I'd stand on my head for a thousand years… for one ten-second glimpse of your beauty…"

They didn't speak on the way home. Nellyanne got out of the truck, walked to the cabin door and went in. She heard Richard pull away.

The next morning, Nellyanne got up and put on a pot of coffee. She walked through the living room to open the front shutters. Richard was sweeping the front porch, humming "You've Made Me So Very Happy," by Blood, Sweat, and Tears. She never opened the door. That night, she went to close the shutters. The porchlight captured Richard's burly body, sitting quietly on the steps. For the next three days, he was there promptly every morning, sitting motionless on the front steps every night.

The night before departure, Nellyanne lay in bed looking at the ceiling. She tossed and turned, unable to fall asleep. She thought about Richard: his kind, generous smile, his boyish innocence, the tears in his eyes when he told her how beautiful he thought she was, the strong, massive arm that pulled her from the kayak. The pledge of a thousand years! She slid out of bed and walked to the front door. When she opened it, Richard turned to look up at her, then to the second hand of his watch.

"Nine, eight, seven, six, five, four, three, two, one…" He looked back at her with a broad smile. "Thank you, Nellyanne," he said. "That's all I needed…" He slapped both knees and leaned forward to get up. "I'll be headed home now…"

Nellyanne opened the door wider. She slowly removed her flannel robe, pulled her knee-length night shirt up over her head, and tossed it to the side. Richard's eyes grew as big as saucers at the sight of her nude body.

"Ricky," she whispered. "Get in here…"

He turned and fell flat on his face, before standing, dusting himself off, and running into the cabin. Nellyanne stepped to the side and giggled as he passed. She closed and locked the door behind him.

TWENTY

Nellyanne stood, hands on hips, as the taxi pulled away. She turned to look at the cozy domicile left vacant for the past three years. Walking up the winding path, she looked left and right with appreciation for the way the red oaks had blossomed so beautifully. Arriving at the front door, she fumbled nervously through her purse for the keys. Out of the corner of one eye, she realized the welcome mat was gone. Once inside, she took three steps before noticing the still, ominous figure sitting with fingers clasped, forearms resting on the dining room table. His eyes watered as he turned his head slowly. She swallowed while searching for the right words to say.

"I never meant to hurt you…" she spoke softly.

He did not answer, instead rising slowly and reaching for the rifle to his left against the wall. He took it by the stock, cradled it with both hands, brought it to his chest, aimed, and fired…

Nellyanne screamed and sat up in the motel bed.

"What is wrong, my love?" A large, African hand gently touched her left shoulder.

The soothing effect of his presence was all she needed. Sliding to his side of the bed, Nellyanne laid her head on his muscular chest and wrapped her right arm around his waist.

"Oh, Sefu," she said as the tears rolled down her face. "I'm so glad you're here! I had the worst nightmare. I'd been away for some reason. I wasn't driving. Took a taxi home. When I walked in the door, Richard was—"

"Ssssh," he said, rubbing her right shoulder. "It was only a dream. He is not here… Only me, my love. And as long as that is the case, no harm will come to you."

She lowered her hand to caress his right thigh. Sefu gently rolled her over on her back and positioned himself on top of her.

"Believe what I say," he whispered.

Nellyanne looked deeply into his eyes, raising both hands to his tapered sideburns.

"It's not a matter of trust, Sefu," she said solemnly. "This is wrong… We both know it… All of this. I am a married woman! What we are doing is wrong… terribly wrong… and it has to stop. It must stop now before it's too late! We've gone from being illicit lovers to murderers, for Christ's sake!"

"There is no need to panic just yet, my love," said Sefu, stroking her left ear and pushing the loose hairs behind it. "I will be leaving soon, and no one will be the wiser…"

"I have a feeling someone already is," said Nellyanne. "Can't explain it… I just know." She attempted to sit up on her elbows. "I should be getting back… We should check out."

After a brief hesitation, Sefu sighed and began to slowly raise his upper body. Nellyanne felt the pressure of his hardened member between her legs. She gasped and reached for his sculpted derriere to still his motion.

"On second thought," she said, tightening her grip. "Not just yet, Kadett…" She lowered her right hand, placing a firm grip on his now throbbing erection.

Sefu smiled, then leaned forward. Nellyanne raised a curled right index finger to her mouth and bit down. She moaned, feeling the start of massive penetration into an area that had been simmering from the moment he climbed between her legs. Moans became groans, then screams as Nellyanne raised her hips and placed both legs on his shoulders. Sefu growled, wrapping his arms around her thighs as he moved skillfully back and forth, deep within the hungry walls of her hospitable vagina.

CHAPTER

TWENTY-ONE

A white Dodge Ram van stops at the entrance. The driver, a tall, costumed figure exits the vehicle. He looks around, grabs the handle on the cargo door and pulls it open. He lifts what appears to be a black leather cadaver bag over his right shoulder and disappears on the other side of the van. He returns moments later, rolling the empty bag, throws it into the cargo compartment, shuts the door, gets back in the van, and drives off into the night fog.

"Wasn't that a Black Panther costume?" Peter said.

Kellyanne took three steps backward.

"Wait! Jenny, can you go back and zoom in on that license plate?"

"Sure can," she said and rewound the feed. "It's BGH 6247. New York plates. I'll run them now."

Kellyanne paced back and forth, her eyes fixed on the screen. A collective gasp engulfed all in the room but Peter as the name appeared: *Nellyanne Summers*.

"We do this by the book," Kellyanne said after a long pause. "With vests, SWAT team, a sniper contingent, and air support."

"What's that address, Jenny?" Peter said, standing and lifting his coat from the chair.

"Last known address was—"

"4200 East Franklin Lane," Kellyanne interjected. "Let's move!"

Jenny spun around in her chair and gave a thumbs-up as they left the room.

Sirens blared like a national emergency warning system as forces arrived on the scene. Patrol cars parked face-to-face at both intersections. Marksmen calibrated sight gauges for distance and wind from rooftops across the street. Helicopters hovered to provide intel and tactical support. The SWAT van double-parked next to the squad car, sitting in front of the red and tan brick colonial house. Twelve men emerged from its rear dressed in full riot gear. A winding concrete walkway separated two patches of lawn, each with a centered, leafless red oak tree.

Kellyanne released the portable two-way ICOM from her utility belt. "All units in position?"

A series of "ten-fours" responded.

"Alright, standfast. Breach only on my command!"

As she reached for the door handle, Peter grabbed Kellyanne's right arm. "What in the hell are you doing?"

"I've got to do this my way, Peter," she spoke softly. "She's my sister..."

Peter looked over his left shoulder at the deputies, back at her, and dropped his hand. Kellyanne opened the door, put her right arm through the strap of an AR-15, swung it over her shoulder, and walked the serpentine path to the front door. She reached through the gray mist for a gold, bumblebee knocker just below the peep hole and knocked three times. Seconds later, the door opened, parting the cloud to reveal the image standing behind it.

Kellyanne stood rigid, initially, absorbing the visceral impact of looking into the eyes of her sister once again. Although they spoke almost nightly by phone—a promise kept at the request of a dying mother—she hadn't been to the house or actually seen Nellyanne in several years.

Nellyanne finished front-tying her robe before addressing her war-ready reflection, "Kellyanne."

"Nellyanne."

"It's been too long. Please, come in." Nellyanne stepped aside as Kellyanne walked past her. She observed the commotion outside, closed the door and turned around, hands on hips.

"This is not a social call, Nellyanne," said Kellyanne, assuming the same stance.

"Yeah, I gathered that, sis," she said. "Have a seat. Let me hang up the wall unit…"

Nellyanne walked through the spacious living room to the kitchen on the left. The incessant beeping of a dangling receiver stopped as soon as she turned the corner. Several minutes of silence followed. Kellyanne noticed the additions of a six-seat French provincial dining room table, dark brown China hutch, and an eight-piece beige sectional sofa. The old, wooden grandfather clock had been replaced with a modern cylindrical one. A newly installed alabaster fireplace sat below a porcelain mantlepiece against the west wall. On the mantlepiece, two pictures of Nellyanne and a tall, burly, bald man stood on either side of a large, centered, NRA membership plaque.

"Nellyanne, we need to get on with this…" Kellyanne reached for her handcuffs and moved toward the kitchen light.

Outside, the team grew restless.

"It's been thirty minutes," said Fresno. "Something's up."

Peter signaled the bobcats. He, Fresno, and Caine exited the vehicle and joined the strike force as they swarmed the front door. Kellyanne was on her knees, frantically administering chest pumps to her sister's body, sprawled on the living room floor, wearing only an untied, orange, mid-length sun robe, white bra and panties. Her rifle leaned at a thirty-degree angle against the fireplace.

"Things got out of hand," she spoke in short breaths, still pumping. "Call an ambulance! Come on, Nellyanne… Come on!!"

Peter approached her from behind, knelt down, reached around to grab both wrists and pulled back, rocking her while she cried. Fresno called the coroner. Caine called for CSI.

A sweep of the crime scene led to recovery of the DSR-1, perched on a gunrack in the backyard shed. It had been wiped clean of fingerprints. The Black Panther outfit was never found. Richard Glasgow, Nellyanne's husband, was arrested at Mickey's Pub several blocks away and booked on charges of illegal possession of an assault weapon and suspicion of first-degree murder. Glasgow would eventually admit to having knowledge of the crime, but maintained it was Nellyanne who pulled the trigger. He would be convicted as an accomplice and sentenced—fifteen years to life.

TWENTY-TWO

The ride back to the precinct was solemn. Fresno and Caine sat in the back seat, eyes closed, ties loosened, bulletproof vests stowed. Peter drove, believing it was the right thing to do. Kellyanne sat stoic, peering out the passenger side window at everything—seeing nothing. She contemplated the upcoming protocol requirements: mandatory bereavement leave, psychiatric counseling, an internal affairs investigation. Peter glanced frequently in her direction, knowing there was nothing he could do to make her feel better. Despite the circumstances, he couldn't help but notice, once again, how beautiful she was. But Kellyanne's thoughts were drifting a million miles away...

The elevator stopped, bobbing up and down at the destination before settling on the third floor. She walked the long, barren hallway to apartment 3G and knocked three times. A distraught Officer Williams answered the door. He looked his partner up and down. His eyes narrowed. He did not speak.

"Are you gonna let me in, or shall I take a seat right here in the hallway?" she said.

He gathered himself, opened the door wider, and stepped aside.

"Sorry… Come on in," he said, closing it slowly behind her.

He motioned to the burgundy love seat in the living room and walked the rectangular runner to the glazed mahogany dining room table. Summers took a seat and watched him lift a tall bottle of red wine to pour himself a glass.

"Can I offer you a drink?" he said, stopping at the three-quarter mark.

"No, thanks," she said with pursed lips. "Where were you? I sat in Jenny's Place for an hour waiting."

"Yeah… I got distracted," he said, taking a moment to raise the glass and swallow twice.

"Come on, Bernie. What was so important that you couldn't give me a heads up?" She noticed the bouquet of red roses laying against an arm of the living room sofa. "Don't tell me you left me hanging for a booty call? I can't believe you would—"

"Got a call from the precinct, Kellyanne," he said, aiming his left palm in her direction. "It was Captain Grant. Got some intel after the last bust."

"The Matatones?"

"Yes. He wants to ship me out to another precinct for a while."

"Why?"

"Apparently, there's a bounty on my head," he said. "Got a little rough slapping the handcuffs on Alessandro… He remembered me."

Kellyanne moved to the edge of her seat. Bernie pulled one of the table's chairs out and sat down.

"He's concerned about it." He placed both arms behind the chair, clasped his fingers and stretched.

Kellyanne stood and walked over to him. She put her right hand on his left shoulder and looked at the wine bottle.

"Where are your glasses?" she whispered.

"In the kitchen. Third cabinet on your right."

She returned and poured a glass. She pulled the chair out next to him, turned and faced him.

"So what did you tell him?" she said.

"Told him we've been at this for nearly four years now. Been threatened before. We don't run from thugs." He leaned forward to pick up his glass.

"You're damned straight, we don't," said Kellyanne. "We take Matatones by the cojones!"

They both burst into laughter.

But Bernie quickly composed himself."I don't know, Kellyanne," he said, shaking his head. "Grant was pretty adamant. He's taking this seriously. Wants to see us both first thing in the morning to discuss the details…"

"So we'll talk!" she said. "Convince him we can handle this. Keep our eyes open and Glocks loaded. Nobody knows these fuckers better than we do, Bernie. You know that. We shouldn't run. That's exactly what they want. We take the fight to them. We cover our own asses, and we put these assholes out of business! Come on, Bernie. What do you say? We gonna punk out or fight?"

Bernie looked at her. A wry smile grew broad and robust. He lifted his glass. "We fight, partner!"

"Damned straight!"

Their glasses clinked as they came together.

Time passed. Two bottles later, they found themselves reminiscing over the time working together. Bouts with The Latin Kings, Nietas, Rat Hunters, and Zulu Nation. Arguing about who saved whose ass more times and achievements deserving of medals that were never awarded. Identifying each other's strengths and weaknesses for the purpose of awareness moving forward.

Kellyanne sat back in her chair, took a deep breath, and looked away from him with a shy smile.

"You know," she said. "I had a terrible crush on you from the day we met at the range." She placed her glass on the table and looked at it. "When the captain paired us up, I banished the thought, though…"

Her eyes shifted to the bouquet on the sofa.

"Feels awkward to mention this now," she said. "It's no longer an issue, and I'm sure you have things going on in your personal life…"

Bernie put his glass down, looked over at the flowers and smiled.

"Funny. I felt the same way when I met you," he said. "But an unwritten law kept me in check."

"What was that?"

"Never dip your pen in the company ink," he said with conviction.

"Oh, that one…"

They sat in silence for several minutes. Finally, Bernie stood.

"It's getting late," he said, reaching for both glasses. "We've got a big day tomorrow. As much as I've enjoyed your company, I think we ought to call it a night."

He disappeared with both glasses and the wine bottle into the kitchen. When he returned, she had not moved.

"Oh no!" she said, sitting upright in the chair and expanding her chest. "Your life is in danger. I'm your partner, and I'm not letting you out of my sight until we get to the bottom of this." She looked once again at the sofa. "Now if you'll bring me a blanket, I'll be quite comfortable over there."

Bernie stood silent, started to speak, but then thought better of it. He walked past the living room into the master bedroom and returned moments later with a thick, suede queen comforter, folded with a pillow and a full-length Mickey Mouse shirt on top of it.

"Will this be sufficient?" he said, tentatively.

"This will be just fine, thank you," she said, standing, accepting the items and walking over to the sofa. She sat them down on one end of it, moved the roses to the coffee table, and turned with hands on hips.

Bernie looked down, turned and walked back to the bedroom door. He turned one last time to look at her.

"By the way," he said. "I'm not seeing anybody right now." He looked at the flowers. "I was going to bring them to Jenny's tonight… They're for you… " He smiled and closed the door.

The next morning, Bernie sang "We Both Deserve Each Other's Love," by LTD, as he rotated his body for final rinsing before stepping out of the shower. When he opened the sliding glass door, there stood a smiling Kellyanne, naked, holding a large drying towel in her right hand.

"Sir, you inquired about our deluxe amenities package along with the possibility of a late check-out?" Her eyelashes batted twice.

She looked down to watch the object between his legs grow closer and closer, forming a perfect right angle to the bathroom floor.

"Bonjour, monsieur," she said, pretending not to be amazed. "Perfect timing… This is a bit heavy…" She draped the towel over the extension that supported it as well as the metal holder it came from.

She giggled as two strong Wakandan warrior hands lifted her off the floor and into the steamed enclosure…

TWENTY-THREE

Arriving at the precinct, the team walked up the stairs in silence. Peter held the front door open for Kellyanne and the deputies. Captain Grant stood in his office doorway; eyes fixed on Kellyanne. She looked down and moved toward him. She entered and he closed the door. Fresno and Caine walked to their respective desks and sat down. Peter went back to the seat next to Kellyanne's.

He reached across the surface to straighten her notepad and pen before noticing Fresno and Caine standing in front of him.

"So what's the plan?" said Fresno, with folded arms.

"Plan?" said Peter.

"Yes, sir," said Caine. "For Detective Summers."

"Can't say that I have one," said Peter, adjusting his tie. "You guys know her better than me… I'm open to suggestions…"

The deputies looked at each other, located two chairs at the desk across from Kellyanne's, rolled them over and sat down.

"Not sure about how they do things back at the nineteenth," said Fresno. "But down here, we step up when the need arises…"

"Like I said," Peter reiterated. "I'm open to suggestions. What do you guys think we should do?"

The deputies exchanged another glance.

"This is not a *we* thing, sir," said Caine, leaning forward. "Deputies cover deputies. Protocol dictates we stay in our own lanes when it comes to something like this. Afraid you'll have to take the lead on this one, Detective Castellano."

Peter shrugged his shoulders. "I barely know her," said Peter. "Besides, she hasn't asked for anything…"

"Does she really have to?" said Fresno.

"We're not talking about your run-of-the-mill botched arrest and apprehension attempt, here," he said. "This was her sister…"

The conversation ceased when the office door opened. Kellyanne emerged alone and closed it quietly behind her.

She turned and walked toward her desk, reserved and poised. Peter watched as she looked down at the rearranged notepad, gathered her belongings, rolled her chair back into place and addressed the team.

"I'm going to be out-of-pocket for a minute," she said. "Bobby, Ricky, I expect you to give Detective Castellano your full support in my absence…"

They nodded. She looked at her new partner.

"Peter, sorry it has to be this way, but the ball's in your court now," she said. "I want you to relax and trust your instincts. You'll be working with two of the finest deputies in the Thirteenth Precinct. They won't let you down. If you need me, I'm just a phone call away…"

Peter nodded, stood and straightened his tie.

Kellyanne walked around the desk, patted Peter twice on the right shoulder and walked out the front door. Fresno and Caine stood, walked across the room to retrieve their coats, and looked back at Peter while putting them on. There would be no next-day briefing. All that needed to be said had already been spoken. Tomorrow would take care of itself. Sudden change, and the need to make adjustments, was part of the job. The three men shared a look of mutual understanding as the deputies left the room.

CHAPTER
TWENTY-FOUR

"**Y**ou didn't have to follow me home, Peter," Kellyanne said, as she unlocked the front door of her brownstone apartment.

"We never got a chance to talk before you left the precinct, Kellyanne," he said, walking in behind her. He stepped aside, as she reached past him to close the door and turn the thumb latch. "I want to know how you're doing…"

"I'm fine," she said, as she walked the long, rectangular, green and white shag runner to the glazed mahogany dining room table. "Just need to take some time to clear my head, you know. The leave will do me good…"

"You cannot be fine after the day you've had!" Peter insisted. "Nobody could…" He walked over to the burgundy, fung shui love seat, sat down, and looked at her.

She tossed her purse and watched it slide to the center of the table, two feet beneath the crystal chandelier. She whirled around with a look as if he'd called her "Kelly."

"What are you, my shrink?" she said, with hands on hips. "Who are you to assume the right to get into my head? Or is this just another character in this one-man play you've been performing all day? Big brother at the crime scene; chauffeur back to the precinct; bell hop at the main house door? Who is the one that followed me home, Peter? The loyal confidante?" She inhaled, exhaled and folded her arms.

"Somebody you can talk to," he whispered. "Don't keep this inside, Kellyanne. I've seen what that can do to partners. You can use me…"

"I am not Stephanie!" she exclaimed, dropping her arms and taking two steps toward him with clenched fists.

"And I am not Bernie!" he said, standing and moving toward her. "You need somebody now. Right now. I am here, damnit! Here for *you*…"

They both stood, frozen, locked in the grip of an uncompromising stare. Tears began to roll down her cheeks. His eyes watered. They stumbled into each other's arms. Kellyanne wrapped both arms around his neck. His arms encircled her waist.

She spoke through lips that trembled, "I killed my sister today… She's gone… What am I going to do?" She moved her arms to hold his face in both hands. "Tell me, Peter… What am I supposed—"

He silenced her with a deep, passionate kiss.

A tsunami of pent-up emotion overtook them. The magnetic field that threatened to disrupt desires to orbit independently, refusing to allow anyone else close enough to heal their losses. The guilt from recognizing that someone can. Smoldering ash, set ablaze by the kindling of today's unthinkable events. Nellyanne's death was the proverbial straw that broke the camel's back.

Kellyanne's tongue found Peter's, as she attacked the buttons on his coat. Peter dropped both arms to let it fall, then reached for the buttons on her blouse. The remaining articles of clothing fell haphazardly around the room, until they stood naked before each other. Peter took a moment to marvel at the unveiled masterpiece. More beautiful than he could have ever imagined, her round, full breasts and jutting nipples heaved with every breath. Her tight stomach drew his attention to the neatly trimmed, wavy black triangle between her thighs. She looked down at his engorged member. Her eyelashes batted.

She looked up, then deeply into his eyes. "I *do* need you, Peter," she whispered. "I need you now…"

She took him by the hand to the bedroom down the hall, just a few feet away.

Hallway lighting illuminated the queen-sized, ebony poster bed. From either side, together they pulled back the ivory rose comforter and crisp, white top sheet, then climbed in. She moved right to left—he, left to right—as they met in the middle.

Peter kissed her gently on the lips. His tongue traveled down her neck to her breasts, drawing circles around the areolas, biting and sucking each nipple. He then brought her breasts together, sucking both nipples at once. She groaned loudly, running her chin, then the right side of her face across the soft, top layer of his silky curls. Her fingers gripped the back of his head, pulling him deeper into her bosom. She let go, moving her hands to his shoulders, as he began the journey south.

He licked, sucked, and nibbled the underside of her breasts, abdomen, and pelvis, ending with long, smooth tongue strokes of the labia. Kellyanne's entire body shook when he took her vulva into his mouth and began to move his head with a slow, steady circular motion. Her toes curled, gripping the fitting sheet at his waist. Her knees stiffened, as she used both hands, working his head to increase rotational speed. Every nerve in her body sensed the rumblings of a heart-stopping orgasm.

Peter stopped suddenly, leaving her gyrating, trembling, and gasping for air. She glared at him with eyes that questioned his timing! Instead, he smiled, rose, took hold of her hips, and turned her over on her left side. He positioned himself behind her and entered with one deliberate motion. Her vaginal walls stretched to accommodate the snug, full fit. She uttered a deep, guttural sound, pressing her cheeks further into his lap.

Kellyanne moved quickly to establish a rhythm.

But Peter grabbed her hips. "Don't move!" he said, holding her firmly.

Kellyanne squirmed uncontrollably, as wave after wave of mounting pleasure engulfed her. She could feel her heart pounding, her breathing accelerated, the tip of his pulsating member at a depth unexplored by anyone before him. She grabbed his right hand and brought his index and middle fingers to her mouth. She then lowered them between her legs, positioning one on each labial lip.

He massaged the folds of soft, malleable skin along the girth of his shaft. She moistened the fingers of her right hand and brought them down to her throbbing clitoris.

Masturbating herself to fever pitch, she had only one request, "Peter...I want to move...Oh, God..."

"Not yet…" he said, increasing his finger tempo.

"Please, Peter…" she said, spanking and frantically rubbing faster. "Ooohhh! Work it! Work me! God, you're so deep… So good… SO FUCK-ING GOOD! I can't wait… OH, GOD… OH, GOD! I… CAN'T… WAIT! I… HAVE… TO… MOVE… NOW… PETER! OOOOOOHHHHHH!"

"Yes! Now!"

He released his grip just enough to give her the freedom she needed. She propelled herself repeatedly into and away from him with the force of a wild, bucking rodeo bronco. He met every thrust with a crashing one of his own. She felt the powerful rush of semen fill her vagina, heard the distant sound of his scream—muffled by her own—just before losing consciousness…

Kellyanne awakened from what must have been one hell of a dream. She released the grip on her pillow, rolled over and looked to the right side of the bed. It had been neatly restored to its original condition. She sat up with her back against the crushed velvet headboard, whisked loose strands of hair behind each ear, and looked at the glass-top, bamboo nightstand to her left. A sixteen-ounce, styrofoam Starbucks coffee cup was sitting there with a note beside it. She picked up the note and read it.

"Thank you for an unforgettable night. You were amazing. I feel like a new man! Call you soon. Have a wonderful day… Peter"

Kellyanne raised both hands to the sky. A childish giggle escaped her lips. She lowered her arms, kissed the note, and exhaled. Yesterday was a terrible—but somehow distant—memory. She couldn't remember the last time she felt this way. Satiated—relieved—happy. She leaned to lay the note next to his pillow, straightened up, raised both knees to her chest, smiled and reached for the cappuccino…

CHAPTER

TWENTY-FIVE

Sefu parked the van in the driveway, grabbed a long, black leather bag, got out and walked to the front door. He slipped the keys under the door mat, along with a white envelope. He raised his cell phone to dial seventeen digits.

"My work here is done, sir," he said as the taxi arrived curbside. "Enroute to the airport. ETA is fifteen minutes." He lowered the phone and got into the cab.

"Mr. Hanif going to LaGuardia?" the driver said.

"Yes, please, and thank you." Sefu sat back in his seat, patted his bag, and smiled.

Charlie raced to position the tarp strategically over the body at the entrance to *Brooks Brothers* as the team approached. Peter lifted the border tape as Kellyanne and the deputies ducked to enter the crime scene. The victim lay on her back, palms down, wearing a blue cashmere sweater, blue and white pinstriped mini-skirt, sheer pantyhose and a pair of white espadrilles. The crowd swelled, exceeding sidewalk space capacity, as news spread quickly of another tragedy in the retail shopping district.

"What've we got here, Charlie?" Kellyanne said, noticing the victim's exposed extremities.

Charlie sprang to his feet, pushed his glasses up the bridge of his nose and cleared his throat.

"Good morning, Detective Summers, Detective Castellano, Deputies Fresno and Caine…" he said. "It's great to have you back, ma'am, by the way. Long three weeks without you. Hope you're feeling better. So sorry for your loss…"

"Thank you, Charlie," she said after exhaling. "What can you tell us about the victim?"

She noted the lack of elevation in the area of tarp where the head should have been.

"Certainly," said Charlie. "Looks like we've got a Sleepy Hollow situation here. Preliminary cause of death appears to be decapitation. Pattern around the point of separation indicates catastrophic impact, removing the head completely. Blood smearing suggests she was killed somewhere else, brought here soon afterward and dragged to this door. I put time of death somewhere between two and four am. Caucasian female, but without dentition, I won't have a clear estimation of age until I examine the bones more closely back at the lab. No personal effects."

"Any idea on the weapon?" she said, walking the length of the body.

"Flash burn and residue on the clothing will give me a better idea of the weapon used. Looks to be a high-powered rifle."

Peter moved closer to the body. "Think I know who this is, Charlie," he said. "You can confirm later, but I believe this is Helen Pace, the cheerleader's best friend."

"How do you get there without a head?" Kellyanne said, looking more closely at the victim.

Peter bent down on one knee to point to the top of the left hand, then looked up at Kellyanne.

They both spoke in unison: "Heart of a Lion…"

"Take a look at the stamp on the underside…" Charlie said, tossing him a pair of latex gloves. Peter put them on and turned the hand over.

"Paris Blues…" All three simultaneously confirmed the connection…

TWENTY-SIX

"**D**etectives Summers and Castellano! A word?"

The billowing voice that rang clearly through the open office door may as well have come from a fire-breathing dragon. When they entered, Captain Grant pointed at two chairs placed directly in front of his desk.

"Have a seat…"

They did.

"I've got a dead body in the middle of my jurisdiction for the second time in as many months. Columbia University has banned all students from nightclubs within a fifty-mile radius. Harlem residents are whispering about 'The Harlem Hunter'. Nationalities are pointing at each other over the killing of 'white girls'. News media's talk of a copycat murderer is stoking fear in the community over the inability of the NYPD to protect its citizens. The mayor's head is so far up my ass I'm constipated… Somebody had better tell me what the hell is going on!'" he said, leaning forward with elbows on his desk, fingers clasped, and chin resting on both thumbs.

"Sir, if I may…" Peter looked at Kellyanne.

She nodded.

He looked back at Captain Grant. "Judging by what we have so far, sir, there is nothing either of us can give you that might sway public opinion or counter the narrative the media is trying to establish," he said. "Both victims were killed somewhere else and brought to Manhattan's shopping district. Both were presumably young, Caucasian women, wearing Columbia school colors. They'd been to Harlem, to the same jazz club—Paris Blues—and a tattoo on this victim suggests she may have been Judith Anderson's close friend, Helen Pace. Tailor-made for the storyline it has created."

"A copycat?" said Grant.

"Afraid so, sir…" said Peter.

"Well, that's just fucking perfect!" Captain Grant slammed both palms on his desktop and looked to the ceiling.

Peter started to speak, but Kellyanne waved her right hand in his direction.

"I'm not buying it!" She sat upright and expanded her chest.

"What do you mean, Detective?" Captain Grant focused hopeful eyes on Kellyanne.

"I believe we're giving the killer too much credit, sir," she continued. "There's something more to this than a vendetta against pom-poms and school spirit. Something more visceral…" She leaned forward. "Judith Anderson was shot in the chest—center mass," she spoke softly, but deliberately. "This victim was decapitated—a shot requiring a much higher level of proficiency. If both victims knew each other, that negates the thought of a random killing—a mere copycat murder. It speaks to reason—purpose—planning—a signature statement from the killer."

"But it makes sense," Grant insisted. "The colors, the shopping district, use of a high-powered weapon, the trip to the night club… It's all—"

"A smokescreen, sir," said Kellyanne. "Colors alone may be attributed to the school. This victim wasn't wearing a cheerleader outfit. Both bodies were brought to our retail shopping district but placed at the entrance of different stores—Dolce and Gabana and Brooks Brothers."

"So what do you make of both girls visiting the same night club the night of the murder? A coincidence?" said Grant.

"Helen Pace made a point of emphasizing the fact that Judith '*raved* about' Paris Blues—a club she and her boyfriend, Jarrod, frequented. She never mentioned going there herself. Sir, this place doesn't strike me as a typical hangout for a Columbia female student… Especially after one of their own was reported to have been there the night she died. We need Charlie to give us a weapon and nail down this victim's identity before drawing any further conclusions…."

"I agree," said Grant. "I'll have forensics put a rush on things. If this turns out to be Helen Pace, dig into her personal life. The connection she shared with Judith likely led to her death. At minimum, there's a killer out there with intimate knowledge of Anderson's murder. Find him or her before the next one!"

"Yes sir!" Both detectives spoke in unison as they left the office.

TWENTY-SEVEN

Helen Pace marched circles around the Lion's insignia on her oval, tweed area rug. The once cozy dorm room now felt claustrophobic. Holding the phone with sweaty palms was a challenge.

"Please, Jarrod," she said. "You're the only one I can talk to… The only person that knew her like I did. I need to find a way to make sense of all this… ." She switched the phone to her left ear and sat at the desk. She picked up a black fountain pen and positioned the square, monogrammed notepad. "Okay… Line six to Falconcrest… And you'll meet me at the station? Thank you so much!"

Jarrod Kitchens never understood the rationale behind grief. Spending valuable time feeling miserable about something you can't do a damned thing about. "Loss in life is a constant—inevitable," his dad would always say. "Tears are a waste of lacrimal gland—designed to clean, nourish, and lubricate the eye, rather than stream aimlessly down one's face. Words alone are insufficient because there are no real answers. The more we talk about it, the worse we feel…" A philosophy to live by, Jarrod thought—until Judith…

Judith embraced loss. She grieved and loved with equal passion. She cried after losing every basketball game. When another underprivileged student lost a bid for scholarship. Hearing gossip of a classmate's stress-induced miscarriage. The time Jarrod failed a midterm she helped him prepare for.

She loved her parents. In spite of their beliefs, she loved Jarrod. She loved the Columbia Lions men's basketball team. And she loved Helen. The least he could do was meet with her—for Judith.

The courtesy hug at the station was brief. Having dinner at Fonda Boricua seemed to be the perfect way to break the ice and start the healing process.

"What's good here?" Helen said, squinting at the menu while reaching for her glasses.

"Judy loved the carne guisada," Jarrod said. "I usually order the bistec encebollado. The homemade stew they cook them in is delicious…"

"Sounds good to me," said Helen. "I'll have her favorite, then." She returned the glasses to the white Michael Kors cross-body handbag at her waist.

During the meal, they took turns sharing favorite anecdotes of life with Judith. They laughed until the reality of her death began to sink in. Helen had a curious thought…

"What do you regret not doing the most while she was alive?" She laid her cutlery down and looked at him.

Jarrod did the same and sat back. "Never meeting her parents," he said. "Should've been more creative about that instead of pressuring her to make it happen. She was on the phone with you the last time I called. It kills me to know the last conversation we had was an argument about that very thing…"

"I have to believe if they'd seen the way you two were together, they would've changed their minds," Helen said with a headshake. "Hell, Stevie Wonder could see you guys belonged together!"

They laughed so hard; people turned their heads.

"What about you? Any regrets?" said Jarrod.

"I regret not seeing Paris Blues."

"Why haven't you?"

"Oh, I don't know… Didn't want to intrude on the time you had together, I guess."

"Well, we can fix that. Let's go tonight…"

"Tonight? You sure?"

"Absolutely! We're both dressed for it. We'll toast to yesterday…"

"I'd like that very much!"

Inside the large, concave room, Helen took Jarrod's left arm to calm her unexpected nerves. Plush, velvet booths for two and four lined the mirrored walls. Couples of every race, creed, and color gathered to celebrate a universal love of jazz. A much higher level of diversity than she would've imagined. An oblong, ivory dance floor spanned three-quarters of the club, from the centered stage to the coat and hat check stand near the entrance. Just As Nice, a Monterey, California band, serenaded the audience with popular requests.

They found a booth for two with a candelabra woven into a white silk tablecloth and ordered drinks—he, a Johnny Walker Black and Coke—she, a Tequila Sunrise. As the night progressed, they laughed, joked, and danced like old friends.

Immediately after last call, the lead singer approached the microphone.

"Ladies and gentlemen, club owners, Vincente and Eva Dubois, have informed us a longtime patron is no longer with us. They've asked that we end this night with a dedication to her…So Judith Anderson, this one's for you," he said as a female bandmember joined him center stage.

The lights went dim as he sang the first line of "One Sweet Day," by Mariah Carey and Boyz II Men: *"Sorry, I never told you all I wanted to say…"*

Couples moved to the dance floor. Helen looked tentatively at Jarrod. They stood. He took her by the hand. The lyrics took them to a place neither thought they'd be when the evening began. Helen wrapped her arms around his neck. Jarrod wrapped his around her waist. They moved in rhythm, swaying in a bond of grief, seeking solace in the moment.

"And I know you're shining down on me from Heaven…" Helen sang along, burying her head in his chest.

Jarrod felt the warmth of her tears. Suddenly, the dam broke. They held each other tightly to prevent a total collapse…

No one spoke on the way back to the station. Both longing, but neither willing to take this one step further. Helen exited quickly without saying goodbye. Jarrod pulled away slowly and headed for 106th street. No one saw or heard the shot that lifted her three feet off the ground, nor the direction from whence it came…

CHAPTER

TWENTY-EIGHT

The jiggling of handcuffs. A frozen shadow splayed left to right across the bright linoleum floor. A shooting pain from head to toe. Waking up under florescent lights in a bed built for one. The tall, dark-haired man with big, bushy eyebrows who approached the side rails and pushed a button, raising her head and neck.

"Good morning," he said with a voice that seemed to echo. "Glad to see you're awake. Do you know who you are? Where you are?"

No answer.

"That's okay… Nod for yes, shake your head for no. Are you experiencing any pain or discomfort?"

A headshake.

"Do you know where you are?"

Another headshake.

"You are in Vivantes Hospital AM Urban, Berlin, Germany. You've suffered severe trauma to the throat, chest, and abdominal region. Stopped breathing three times, requiring resuscitation and emergency surgery upon arrival." He moved closer. "I need you to blink for the number of fingers I'm holding up…"

Two blinks.

"Good. Now follow my finger moving just your eyes…"

Eyes moved right to left, left to right, up and down.

"Very good! There seems to be no evidence of brain damage. Do you have an appetite?"

One nod.

"Excellent! Let's get you fed. It'll be a liquid diet until you're well enough. I'm Doctor Michael Shaughnessy, your attending physician. I'll be back to take another look at you sometime this afternoon. You're going to be just fine."

He smiled and took one step to his left. A short, balding man with blonde eyebrows stepped forward. He smiled with gold-capped teeth lining his upper row.

"This is Dean Lenholtz," said Dr. Shaughnessy. "It is he who made arrangements for you to be treated here. I'll leave the two of you alone…" He bowed, turned, and left.

"It is so good to see you again, Lehrer Summers," the man spoke with a heavy east German accent. "We received your distress call. Got there as soon as we could. We were able to make the switch on the causeway and reroute you to the airport. The coroner's staff was sedated and unharmed. They will awaken with no recollection of prior events. Our technicians did a great job keeping you alive until we could give you the care you needed. Once you have fully recovered, we will come for you and discuss the future. You have been sorely missed…"

CHAPTER

TWENTY-NINE

Charlie sat with his index and middle fingers touching his cheek, thumb under chin, right elbow on the reading desk. The gun manual lay open at the centerfold. He did not see Kellyanne and Peter walk in.

"What do you have for us, Charlie?" Kellyanne said.

"Hello, detectives," said Charlie. "I received confirmation on the victim and the murder weapon." He removed his glasses, sat back and rubbed his eyes.

"Helen Pace?"

"It is."

"And the weapon?"

Charlie stood and approached them with the manual. He held it at chest level, with the centerfold facing them. "This is the McMillan Tac-50 long range sniper rifle," he said. "Roughly five feet long, weighs twenty-six pounds and has a thirty-inch barrel. It uses .408 caliber projectiles."

"Yeah," said Peter. "A sniper rifle…Like the one used in the Judith Anderson murder."

"Not exactly, Detective Castellano…"

Charlie handed the book to Peter and began to pace the floor. Kellyanne turned to study the picture with him as Charlie continued.

"This weapon is more powerful," Charlie said, turning to face them with arms folded. "A far more powerful weapon than would be necessary to kill a human being. It is an anti-material weapon, used to destroy *things*, like military equipment, structures, and the like. It was used in the Bosnian war, in Iraq, and Afghanistan. I misinterpreted the pattern at the point of separation as indicative of a ripping away motion resulting from impact. However, the circumference, the burning and melting away of organ tissue, is more indicative of a vicious explosion. Not only was she decapitated, her head was immediately reduced to minute bone and tissue fragments."

"So there would be no head to recover…" Kellyanne said, now with hands on hips.

"None to speak of, I'm afraid."

"How difficult would it be to obtain a weapon like this?" Peter said.

"That's another problem," said Charlie, nodding his head. "It's accessibility. This rifle is made right here in the United States—Phoenix, Arizona—and is distributed worldwide. You'd have to be connected, of course, but Canada, France, Turkey and Israel have all used it in guerilla warfare training. Your killer could be anyone, from anywhere with proper access."

"Looks to me like our shooter wanted more than just to kill," said Kellyanne. "He or she was going for total destruction. A shot that would demonstrate the unique skill of the one who made it. A commercial to validate the weapon's flexibility. This was fucking target practice!"

Kellyanne looked at Charlie, then Peter.

"My thoughts exactly, Detective Summers," said Charlie. "Be careful. This weapon currently holds the record for the longest sniper kill shot from distance. You may be looking for someone who would relish the pursuit. Even challenge you to do so."

Kellyanne took the manual from Peter's hands and pressed the centerfold into Charlie's chest. "Challenge accepted!" She turned to Peter. "Come on, partner. We've got work to do! Thank you, Charlie…"

"Detective Summers!" Charlie lowered the manual. Kellyanne turned to look at him.

"Yes, Charlie," she said.

"I've always admired your resolve…" he said. "And God knows I doubt neither your professional skill, nor your ability to neutralize this threat…" He raised the centerfold facing her once again. "But this weapon blew the head of Helen Pace clear off her body from God only knows how far away. She never saw it coming. Please... Watch your six on this one."

Peter stood silent. He looked at Charlie, then at Kellyanne. She walked over to Charlie to place her right hand on his left shoulder.

"I will, Charlie," she said. "I always appreciate your insight... and your friendship. We'll go as slow as it takes to do this the right way... Thank you." She turned and walked out the door with Peter.

Back at the main house, Fresno and Caine met them at the rear entrance.

"We caught a break on the cam footage," said Caine. "Got a hit on the body dump..." He looked at Fresno.

Fresno put his right hand on Kellyanne's left shoulder. "Brace yourself, ma'am," he said. "This could be a game-changer..."

The van pulled away from the curb, leaving the body laying with feet pointing upward in opposite directions. The room was silent. After verifying the details, Jenny stopped the feed and turned the monitor from view. She looked down as the team left the room.

Kellyanne walked past her desk and out the front door with Peter in hot pursuit. "Kellyanne, wait!"

She wheeled around in tears to face him at the steps. "Peter, please tell me I didn't kill my sister while attempting to arrest her for a crime she did not commit!!"

"You don't know that, Kellyanne..."

"Are you kidding me? It was the same van! The same costume! Glasgow is behind bars and we both know she is dead!"

"Okay, so we go with the only logical explanation—a copycat..."

"Not with the same exact vehicle and license plate, Peter!"

"Maybe it's like the captain said. Someone with intimate knowledge—"

"Those details were never released to the public," she interjected. "Look, we know the Black Panther costume was never recovered. The only thing we have is Glasgow's statement that Nellyanne pulled the trigger."

Peter looked away momentarily, then back at Kellyanne, who was now standing with hands on hips.

"And if he knows Nellyanne is innocent, why would he implicate his own wife?" Peter said.

He turned toward the door with raised eyebrows. She followed him back inside.

THIRTY

"Hey, Jimmy," Peter spoke over the telephone at his newly assigned desk. "Yes, we traced her actions that night to *Paris Blues* and to the guy witnesses say she was with—Jarrod Kitchens. He cooperated fully, giving us access to his apartment, automobile and DNA. Went through his financials with a fine-toothed comb. We came up empty. Nothing to suggest he had the means, motive, or skill to pull off a crime of this magnitude. Keep working on it from your end, though. I'll let you know if we come up with something here. Thanks, brother…"

He hung up and turned to Kellyanne, who'd pulled up a chair next to the desk as Fresno and Caine approached.

"Hey, fellas," said Peter. "Anything on the weapon?"

"Nothing out of the ordinary," said Caine, looking at his notepad. "Ten shipments in the last six months to Coronado and Little Creek, pegged for the Navy Seals. Seven to Canada, three to Israel and one to Germany."

"Hmmm," Peter said, reaching for the notepad. "Germany wasn't on the list of primary users Charlie mentioned." He handed the notepad back to Caine. "See if you can track down the consignee for that particular shipment before diving deeper into the rest."

Kellyanne tapped her fingers on the desk as she watched them leave. "We're gonna get this bastard…" she said. She looked at Peter with raised eyebrows. "You know, I have to say, I'm very impressed with your instincts. They were foolish to let you go."

"I disagree," he said. "Seems that decision came with some insight. This is exactly what I needed. To be part of something again. To be the other half of a whole. A union that fits, you know…"

Kellyanne smiled and looked around. "Uuummm," she purred. "Well, you definitely fit…"

Peter winced and looked around. He looked back at Kellyanne with narrowed eyes. "Kellyanne," he whispered with a smile. "I think we should be more careful…"

Kellyanne shrugged her shoulders. "Relax, Peter," she said. "Everyone knows we're partners now. They like the fact that we seem to be getting along. It's difficult to replace the bond you had with a previous partner."

Peter nodded.

"I guess you're right," he said. He sat back in his chair as thoughts shifted to another subject. "Speaking of lost connections… How are you doing? Anymore nightmares about Nellyanne?" He hoped he hadn't spoken too soon.

Kellyanne sighed. "I'm managing," she said, looking away briefly. "The job keeps me busy during the day… And I sleep like a baby at night." She looked back at Peter and smiled broadly. "I honestly don't know what I would've done without you…"

"I feel the same way," he said. "It's as if a guardian angel swooped down to fulfill both our needs."

"Divine intervention," she said. "I like the sound of that… Something I'll always be thankful for…"

He smiled and leaned closer. "And speaking of needs…"

They shared a knowing look.

She scanned the room before whispering in his direction, "Meet me in the utility restroom. They leave it for me, Jenny, and Jamie. Neither of them ever uses it…" She stood, smiled, and walked away.

Peter watched the seconds tick away on his silver Tag Heuer. At the three-minute mark, he looked around, stood, and walked to the dark, narrow passageway left of the janitorial equipment. He opened the door at the far end, immediately noticing the black pumps draped in red panties on the floor behind the closed stall. When it opened, ever-so-slowly, he smiled and entered, closing the door behind him. The sounds of a belt buckle and zipper bounced off the bright, porcelain-tiled walls. His pants and briefs dropped to his ankles. He gasped as softly as he could. The pump heels rose and descended in rhythm, but the toes remained planted firmly on the floor…

THIRTY-ONE

The orange jumpsuit-clad lumberjack entered the 4X4 foot cubicle, head up, eyes wide open, smiling with a mouth full of half-rotten teeth. He had not had a visitor since incarceration. Even a chance to talk to cops was a welcomed diversion. Or so he thought—until he looked into the fortified glass window at Kellyanne. His eyes narrowed, the smile disappeared, going from frown to full-on scowl.

Peter looked at Kellyanne, sat down and picked up the phone. He tapped it on the window and motioned to Glasgow, who finally sat down to do the same, still glaring at her.

"Mr. Glasgow, look at me," said Peter. "I'm Detective Peter Castellano. This is Detective Kellyanne Summers, whom I presume you recognize. Revisiting your case, sir, we now have reason to believe you were never an accomplice in the crime you were convicted for."

Glasgow turned slowly to Peter. "Never said I was. You people did."

"Yes, and we're working to rectify that mistake," Peter said. "To do that, however, we need you to answer a few questions. Now, did you not admit to having knowledge of the crime committed?"

"I did."

"Does that mean you know who did it?"

"I do."

"Was it Nellyanne, as you stated previously for the record?"

Glasgow would not answer.

"Sir, if you value your freedom, we need to know the truth."

Glasgow remained silent.

"Mr. Glasgow—"

Kellyanne touched Peter's left shoulder.

"Let me talk to him," she said, wiggling her fingers to beckon for the receiver.

Glasgow glanced quickly between the two of them as if in protest. Peter looked up at her, back at Glasgow, stood up and handed her the phone. As she sat down, Glasgow sat back. The scowl returned. Kellyanne leaned forward.

"Mr. Glasgow…Richard," she began softly. "I want you to look at me… Not with your eyes, not with anger, pain, or a thirst for revenge. Remember this face and see me with your heart… Now you are going to spend a very long time in here if we don't have enough to prove your innocence. Did Nellyanne kill that girl or not?"

The scowl slowly disappeared. His lips tightened. His eyes watered.

"No…She did not…" he said, as tears trickled down the sides of his nose. He lowered his head and began to shift left to right in the chair.

Kellyanne looked up at Peter. "It's okay," she said. "I know this is difficult for you. Take a moment if you need to…"

As time passed, the atmosphere changed. The glacier between them began to melt. Their eyes met, generating a bridge of understanding that permeated the glass. Kellyanne raised her left hand to the barrier. His right hand elevated slowly to meet it. The relief in his eyes spoke volumes.

After a couple more minutes, she leaned forward again. "If she did not do this, why did you say she did?"

"Because she might as well have!" His voice was now broken.

"What do you mean?"

"I mean she's the reason that girl is dead."

"Why?" she spoke with a voice that was now elevated, sounding more like a sister than an interviewer. "What did she do or say to cause that girl to be murdered?"

He would not answer.

"Richard, we're going to need more from you," she persisted. "We need to know who the killer is. And if what you say is true, we need to know what role Nellyanne played in all of this!"

He wiped his eyes, sat back and gathered himself.

"I'm done talking," he said calmly.

"Do you understand we cannot help you if you don't?"

"I don't care! Doesn't matter anyway… She's dead, right?"

"Who was the shooter?" Kellyanne exclaimed.

He hung up the phone, stood, and walked away from the glass. He ignored her protests as the guard opened the door for re-entry.

CHAPTER

THIRTY-TWO

Back at the main house, Captain Grant and Deputies Fresno and Caine were having a lively conversation while leaving his office as Kellyanne and Peter entered the building. Grant motioned for silence at the sighting.

"You two are just in time," he said. "Fresno and Caine managed to track down the weapon. The consignee's name is not in the system, but the address is clear." He handed a copy of the shipping label to Kellyanne.

"4200 East Franklin Lane…" She looked back at Grant. "Doesn't make sense," she said. "If this is the address, the receiver should have either been Nellyanne, or Richard. Proof of identification would've been required."

"Exactly," said Grant. "To be authorized access to a shipment like this, Sefu Hanif is in somebody's database. Don't worry, we'll find him. But it gets better… I just received a call promising to break this case wide open. On our way to the onsite interview right now. You guys up for a quick trip uptown?"

"Sure, Captain," said Peter, adjusting his tie. "Where're we going?"

"Columbia University. The caller will meet us there…"

They followed him out the front door.

Admissions was visible just past the lobby after the automatic glass doors. A young, blonde receptionist smiled as Captain Grant approached the counter.

"Hello. I'm Captain Grant of the New York City Police Department. These are Detectives Summers and Castellano, Deputies Fresno and Caine. We're here to conduct an interview—"

"Yes, sir," she said, extending her right arm toward a well-lit corridor. "We've been expecting you. Third door down on your right…"

Her eyes widened as she watched Kellyanne walk away with the team. When they were a safe distance down the hall, she turned to whisper to co-workers seated at desks behind her.

Dean Bollinger, aerial shots of the atrium and campus grounds, and gold-plated wooden plaques for academic excellence lined the sky-blue walls of the Ivy League hallway. When they arrived at the counselor's office, Captain Grant touched Kellyanne's left shoulder.

"Detective Summers," he said. "Why don't you take it from here? You're the best interrogator I have."

She nodded and knocked three times.

"Come in…" The voice from within spoke softly.

They entered in single file: Kellyanne, Peter, Fresno, Caine, then Captain Grant, who closed the door behind them. Several feet from the doorway, a demure figure sat with her back turned at a long, L-shaped black console arranging papers. She wore a blue and white turtleneck sweater. The lower part of her wavy black hair was obstructed by the high-back desk chair. She placed a short stack of papers under a miniature snow globe to her right. The swivel chair rotated slowly counterclockwise, revealing a partially covered left ear, strong jawline, tanned complexion, tapered nose and a widow's peak. Her emerald-green eyes glistened as she whisked the overlapping hair behind her ear and stood, hands on hips. Her nose crinkled when she saw the woman standing nearest to her.

"Nellyanne," she said with pursed lips.

"Kellyanne," came the involuntary response.

"Peter, Ricky, Bobby, Captain Grant…It's so good to see you all again…"

Peter took three steps backward, staring wide-eyed and open-mouthed at the woman he now realized was an imposter! Fresno, Caine and Captain Grant all smiled.

"How did you…" Nellyanne's voice was barely a whisper. "I thought you were… They thought I was—"

"Turned out to be a rash of misunderstandings," said Kellyanne. "You came back to set the record straight. Took up where you left off. It was actually fun. Like the games we used to play when we were kids. So while you were busy being me, I made the most of being you. Oh, by the way, I want to commend you on your meticulous notetaking. The evaluations of both Judith Anderson and Helen Pace were particularly helpful in putting this whole thing together... How did you manage to pull off such a convincing me?"

"I'm a counselor," Nellyanne spoke calmly. "My job is to listen, record, and advise. You talked so much about the job—the people you worked with, your innermost feelings about them—both professionally and emotionally... " She paused to glance at Peer, who looked at her, at Kellyanne, then dropped his head. "I knew it, and them, as well as you do. Why do you think we spoke so often over speakerphone? I was taking notes. We share a rich history of pretending to be one another. Fooling teachers, boyfriends, Daddy—"

"You mean Uncle Jerome," Kellyanne spoke, opening the top right desk drawer to produce a slightly worn, white envelope.

Nellyanne's mouth opened.

"Took the liberty of reading it," Kellyanne continued. "Hope you don't mind. Enlightening... Bit of an emotional roller coaster ride but comforting in the end." She tapped the fingers of her right hand on the face of the envelope. "Guess you forgot Mommy's advice on finding a suitable mate, huh?"

Nellyanne looked to her left. She looked back and shrugged her shoulders. "What can I say?" she said. "I have a dysfunctional need for emotional support... at all costs."

Kellyanne folded her arms with raised eyebrows.

"There's one thing I still don't get," she said. "Captain Grant said you were deeply invested in the solving of both murders..."

"I had no choice, Kellyanne," she said with now watery eyes. "With you gone and Sefu out of the country, I had to do everything in my power to make things right. I did it for my own sanity ...and I did it for you..."

Fresno had heard enough. He turned to Captain Grant, who nodded. The deputy positioned himself behind Nellyanne. She sighed, turned her head slightly to the right, and placed both hands behind her back.

"Nellyanne Summers," he began. "You are under arrest for the murders of Judith Anderson and Helen Pace, the attempted murder of Detective Kellyanne Summers, and for impersonating a New York City Police Detective. You have the right to remain silent. Anything you say—"

"Wait!" said Nellyanne suddenly. She turned 270 degrees to acknowledge Fresno. "Can you give me a minute, please? …Just a minute… I promise…" She turned to look at Kellyanne once more. "You'll never know how happy I am to see that you're still alive, Kellyanne… Sis…"

Fresno released his handcuffs.

"Ricky, wait!" Kellyanne walked around the desk and took several steps until she and Nellyanne were standing face-to-face.

For several moments, they stared into each other's eyes. Nellyanne dropped her hands to her sides, palms forward… Suddenly, they unleashed a primal scream that shook the room, as they fell into each other's arms. From one, a plea for forgiveness—from the other, an outpouring of unconditional compassion. Both remembering, despite their differences, the unbreakable bond between them. The rest of the team formed an empathetic circle around them…

THIRTY-THREE

"So she's alive and in custody?"

"That's right, sir," said Kellyanne. "And if you don't tell us what you know, the D.A. is calling for the death penalty. Her life depends on your decision..."

Glasgow rubbed his head and sat back. He looked at Kellyanne, then at Peter, standing to her left. He pointed his index finger at the faces on the other side of the glass.

"It was him," he growled. "That African nigger she loved. Tried her best to hide it... her feelings... but I always knew. She never loved me..."

Nellyanne entered the quiet conference room in handcuffs and shackles, flanked by a two-man security detail. She immediately noticed three well-dressed professionals already seated at the table ahead: Agents Robert Sorensen of the CIA, Felicia Meyers of the FBI, and Special Officer Steven Loudermilk of the Department of Homeland Security. They stood in courteous silence, as she was seated and relieved of her handcuffs. She acknowledged each one as they sat back down. Nellyanne rubbed her wrists and clasped her fingers on the table. She cleared her throat to begin speaking in accordance with her plea agreement:

"His name is Sefu Hanif. Swahili for 'Sword Believer'." She spoke first in the direction of the African American FBI agent, Ms. Meyers.

"African?" said Meyers.

"Yes. East Africa. He was born in Nairobi, Kenya."

"How did the two of you meet?" said Sorensen.

"He was a foreign exchange student I trained in guerilla warfare tactics while teaching in Germany five years ago."

"Where in Germany?" said Meyers.

"At the Deutsche Spionage Akademie…" Nellyanne spoke to three suddenly blank faces. "It's an isolated, covert institution, located inside a fortified compound on the outskirts of Berlin…"

"How did you come to teach there?" said Sorensen.

"I was recruited by the dean of the school, Helmut Lenholtz, while seeking employment in Berlin. He has a highly trained staff that recruits instructors and students based on specific qualifications."

"And what was his interest in Mr. Hanif?" said Loudermilk.

"Sefu is a trained assassin, who'd attained the ranks of Alama 'Marksman', Mpiganaji 'Combatant', and Mama Muuaji 'Master Killer', in Bloemfontein."

"How did this association result in the commission of two homicides in Manhattan?" said Loudermilk.

"He was my star student," said Nellyanne. "We became close—too close for Sefu. His disdain for American capitalism and interracial couples kept us apart—at least until after I returned to America—to accept a counseling position at Columbia U. We kept in touch, with him visiting frequently on a tourist visa. We fell in love. After I married Richard, he threatened twice to kill him so that we could be together permanently. I continued to see him anyway, but away from my home and husband."

"The murders here, Mrs. Glasgow…" said Loudermilk.

"Yes, of course," she said apologetically. "I confided in him often about pressures on the job. When I mentioned my frustrations with Judith Anderson and Helen Pace in particular, he vowed to resolve both problems."

"What were the frustrations?" said Meyers.

"Judith was willing to throw a very bright future away for a basketball jock," Nellyanne said as she felt tremors of recollections. "Helen followed suit, hoping that Judith would wake up someday and accept the undying love of a lesbian. It drove me crazy…"

"So he did this for you?" said Meyers, with arched eyebrows.

"Yes… He said the death of Judith was proof of his love for me. He would not stop until I considered him worthy of my trust. When I assumed my sister's identity and Richard was arrested, I gave him full access to my house and van so he wouldn't have to incur the expense of lodging and transportation while waiting to see me. Helen Pace was unfortunately the last of two sacrificial lambs—massacred in the name of love…"

Meyers leaned forward to look deeply into Nellyanne's eyes. "Mrs. Glasgow," she said. "How could you let this happen? How could you allow two innocent women to be so senselessly murdered?"

"He did it for me…For love…I had to protect him…"

"Knowing he was a cold-blooded killer?"

Nellyanne's eyes watered. She unclasped her fingers and leaned back in the chair.

"I guess you've never *really* been in love before…"

Air Canada Flight 9537 from LaGuardia to Berlin was on final descent. Despite a period of strong turbulence crossing the Atlantic, the A321 experience was a lovely one. Sefu Hanif closed the latest copy of *Guns and Ammo*, relaxed his eyes, settled into his first-class seat, and thought about the lesson plans for next semester. The coach crowd erupted in applause as wheels touched down. It felt good to be home…

In front of Brandenburg International, a silver and black stretched limousine was parked with the passenger door open. Two men in black, red, and gold uniforms took his luggage and opened the trunk. A tall chauffeur stood at attention by the door. Sefu got in. A smiling Dean Lenholtz handed him a tall, crystal glass of Boërl & Kroft Brut.

"Welcome, Lehrer Hanif," he said with a jubilant smile. "I trust your flight was a pleasant one?"

"It was, sir," said Sefu, eagerly accepting the glass.

"And the business went well?"

"Very well. The deserter and her husband are both incarcerated. Her reputation is ruined. Her life—little as she has left—will never be the same. Your vengeance has been exacted, Meister Lenholtz."

"Were you able to validate the efficiency of the weapons we sent?"

"I was. One shot per kill. The live field experience was invaluable. I am anxious to share my findings with the students this semester. *Gehen* Maneuvers must be updated…In the process, I reaped the spoils of two name-brand satchels from the carcasses—one from Gucci, the other from Michael Kors. I sent them home to my dear mother. She will be delighted!"

"You are a cherished asset, Mr. Hanif. Let us raise a toast…To Mission Erfüllt!"

"Prost!"

Their glasses clinked loudly as the vehicle merged with outgoing traffic…

Nellyanne stood, hands on hips, as the taxi pulled away. She turned to look at the home she'd left vacant for the past three years. Walking up the winding path, she looked left and right with appreciation for the way the red oaks had blossomed so beautifully. Arriving at the front door, she noticed that the welcome mat was no longer there. She fumbled nervously for her keys. Once inside, she took three steps before noticing the still, ominous figure sitting with fingers clasped, forearms resting on the dining room table. His eyes watered as he turned his head slowly to glare at her. She swallowed while searching for the right words to say.

"I never meant to hurt you…" she spoke softly.

He did not answer, instead rising slowly and reaching for the rifle against the wall nearby. He raised it with both hands, aimed, and fired…

CHAPTER

___

THIRTY-FOUR

"Detective Summers, Castellano… A word?" Captain Grant's tone was significantly lighter than usual.

He opened his office door to reveal a tall, brown-haired man dressed immaculately in a Kelly-green full-service military uniform. His right breast pocket was topped by six full rows of commendations, rank insignia on both shoulders, along his right arm, and a solid-brimmed hat tucked at the elbow. He stood rigid, as if awaiting inspection, before eagerly approaching Kellyanne and Peter.

"Detectives," announced Grant. "Meet Major Heinrich Ballack, commander of the Seventh Regimen, Bundeswehr, Army Division."

Major Ballack shook Peter's hand firmly with his right hand, paused, then took Kellyanne's hand with both hands. His intense gaze made her feel like a distinguished visitor. She was tempted to bow. He then straightened his back, performed a snappy sidestep, marched over to Captain Grant, shook his hand, and walked out of the office. Kellyanne and Peter looked at each other.

"Have a seat, you two," said Grant, pointing to the sofa against the wall. They did…

"What was that all about, sir?" said Peter.

Kellyanne listened, still slightly disoriented as they both sat down. Captain Grant walked behind his desk, sat down, placed both arms on the glass top and leaned forward.

"In ninety days, I'm sending you both to Germany," he spoke with a suddenly solemn voice. "You'll be participating in a joint, multinational anti-espionage effort in Berlin, headed by the man you just met." He sat back and loosened his tie. "I realize this is an unusual turn of events," he admitted. "But the attorney general singled you out. It's out of my hands."

"Us?" said Kellyanne. "Why?"

"I sent the mayor the after action report you completed after your time there, along with an evaluation of the two of you as a team, and the next thing I knew, I was in a huge boardroom talking to a lot of people making a lot more money than me."

"But what about things around here?" said Peter. "We've got important work to do yet, sir."

"I'm aware of the stakeout with the Latin Kings," he said. "It can wait until you get back." He stood. "Gangs come and go. They die, resurrect, new ones develop, they get bigger, stronger, and more organized. They'll keep us busy for quite some time. But this is a chance to put our footprint on punishing the slime that terrorized Manhattan… Can I count on you?"

"Yes sir!" they chimed in unison as they left the office…

Detective Kellyanne Summers sat in an unmarked town car with black tinted windows. She released the portable ICOM from her utility belt.

"All units in position?"

A series of "ten-fours" replied in short succession.

"Eagle and Condor have left the terminal. Proceed with caution. Maintain your distance. I don't want them spooked. Standfast fifty kilometers from the akademie entrance."

A second round of "ten-fours" replied in short succession.

She looked to the right at her now fully vetted sidekick. "You ready, partner?"

Peter smiled, raised his glock-17, pulled and released to charge the chamber, and shouldered it.

"Bet on it," he said.

Kellyanne smiled broadly with renewed appreciation for the wisdom of her mentor, Captain Grant. She shifted the car into gear and merged left into a cavalcade of Bundeswehr army Humvees. The operational tasking was three-fold: to protect the sanctity of diplomatic relations, deliver the one true anti-dote for the venom of vengeance, and exact full-circle justice. Justice for Judith Anderson, Frank and Margaret Anderson, Helen Pace, Ronald and Jasmine Pace, Jarrod Kitchens, Columbia University, the citizens of Manhattan, Harlem, and… for her misguided sister, Nellyanne.

CHAPTER

THIRTY-FIVE

"**F**or acts of bravery above and beyond the call of duty while participating in an international effort to fight espionage, we are honored to present the Silver Shield to Detectives Kellyanne Summers and Peter Castellano."

The conference room erupted with applause as the partners walked across the stage. A smiling Captain Grant shook hands with and hugged them both.

Two weeks later, it was back to business. Summers and Castellano were parked away from the dimly lit parking lot, several feet behind Melinda's Eatery on East 34th Street. Peter was behind the wheel. Kellyanne observed the alley with two large, industrial trash compactors standing against a dingy brick wall.

"You sure it was Melinda's?" said Peter.

"According to intel," said Kellyanne, shrugging her shoulders. "The drop is set for tonight." She glanced at her watch. "Any minute now, as a matter of fact." She whisked loose strands of hair behind each ear.

Peter looked at her and smiled.

"What?" she said, lowering her hands.

"Nothing," he said, looking past her to the alley. He sighed and sat back in the seat. "I just can't get over the resemblance... You know, between the two of you."

Kellyanne turned to look at the spacious alley. She couldn't help but remember the way Nellyanne described their collective tryst during visitations. She wondered why he never mentioned it...

"Yep," she said, choosing not to look at him. "Indistinguishable... but very, very different..."

Peter shifted somewhat to look at her. "I don't know about that. We've been partners for a while now, and I—"

"*Ssshh*," she reached out with her left hand in his direction as four black Jeep Cherokees assembled in the lot, facing each other, two on either side. "Looks like it's about to go down..."

Kellyanne immediately realized she had inadvertently placed her hand on his inner right thigh. The pulse beneath her palm told her it was not an object of government issue. Their eyes locked for several moments, neither one moving, before the sound of closing car doors shattered the trance. They gathered themselves, brandished their weapons, and waited for the exchange.

Four men, one from each Jeep, exited the vehicles wearing black and gold hoodies, with block initials ALKOB. Two of them joined hands, touched elbows, drew each other close, and hugged. One was given a black attaché case by the assistant of the other, while the other accepted a like container from the other assistant. Both assistants returned to their cars empty-handed, starting engines while the spokesmen opened the cases and conversed.

"Fucking Latin Kings," growled Kellyanne. "Call for backup!" As Peter lifted the patrol car's transmitter, Kellyanne exited the car. "NYPD! Drop the cases and put your hands behind your head!"

Two of the Jeeps shifted into gear and with tires spinning, sped away from the scene. The spokesmen each lowered their respective packages and lifted their hands. As Kellyanne moved closer, the facial features of the one on the right made her stop where she stood in disbelief.

"Sonny-Boy?"

"Kellyanne?" he said, smiling broadly. "You a cop?"

His sweet, unassuming voice put her in a time machine, carrying her back to a college dorm room light years away...

"Will it hurt, Sonny?" she said, breaking the thread of their intertwined tongues and pushing his chest.

"It's gonna be fine, baby," he said pressing forward. But she resisted.

"I want to see it first," she said, sitting up on both elbows.

Sonny-Boy sighed, then sat up proudly on his knees. Kellyanne gasped at the revelation.

"That is gonna hurt me, Sonny!" she exclaimed with wide eyes. It was fully three times the length of Tommy's, and nearly twice the girth of her Uncle Jerome's.

Sonny-Boy took both her hands, lowered them to her waist, and stroked her brow. "Don't worry, Kellyanne," he whispered. "We're gonna do this the right way. I need you to trust me, and do exactly as I say… Can you do that, baby?"

Kellyanne exhaled and laid back down on the firm twin bed. "Ok," she whispered. "What do you want me to do?"

"First, close your eyes," he said placing two fingers on both her eyelids. "Now imagine you are alone, thinking about us… What we have… What this would be like… Take a couple of deep breaths…"

She did.

"I'm kissing you… Touching your breasts… Pinching your nipples…"

The image in her mind was crystal clear.

"Now I want you to play with yourself… Slowly…"

She lowered her right hand in obedience. Fluid seeping from the tip of his member at her orifice lubricated the underside of her fingers. Her rhythm increased. Her breathing quickened. She felt the head move slowly past her labial folds. A searing pain ensued.

"Sonny!"

He stopped. After a while, the pain subsided, but unspeakable pleasure took its place. With eyes still closed, she nodded. Another inch, then two, and the pain returned. When she clenched her teeth, Sonny stopped. This went on until he was three-quarters of the way in. At this point, the pain had lessened and, aided by her own fevered masturbation, the pleasure had reached a height she'd never known.

"Sonny!" she screamed, grabbing his butt and pulling him to the point of no return.

Sonny moved back and forth, sending earthquake tremors from her head to her toes. She wrapped both legs around his waist, raising and lowering to meet every thrust.

"OH GOD! OH JESUS! SONNY! SONNY! SONNY!"

Kellyanne distinctly remembered having three mind-blowing orgasms before Sonny screamed and joined her for the last.

She'd never forgotten that night… nor him…

CHAPTER

THIRTY-SIX

"**K**ellyanne? You ok?" His voice brought her back to the reality of the moment.

Kellyanne was suddenly aware she had lowered her weapon, while Sonny-Boy was holding a .44 Magnum aimed directly at her head. She blinked twice and gathered herself.

"Drop the weapon, Sonny!" she said. "Drop it now!"

"Afraid I can't do that, baby," he said, flashing a wry grin. "Gonna have to leave you here and finish my business..."

"I don't want to do this, Sonny," she said with watery eyes. "Don't make me do this... I'm not going to ask you again. Now drop your weapon, or—"

"Or what, baby? You'll shoot me?" he spoke, taking a step toward her. "I know you wouldn't do that... Not my *Kama Sutra* queen...Look at you...All flushed and teary-eyed. This is gonna hurt me more than you'll ever know... " He raised the gun a little higher.

Kellyanne stood frozen.

The bullet that landed center forehead originated six feet behind her. As Sonny-Boy fell to the ground, the other gang member dropped to his knees, placing both hands behind his head. Kellyanne turned to look at Peter, who stood ready to fire again if needed. She pursed her lips, whirled around, stepped over Sonny-Boy's body, and walked over to handcuff the remaining Latin King. Sirens blaring in the distance signaled the arrival of reinforcements.

The late-night ride back to the precinct was pensive. Both minds whirling in uncertainty over the night's events. Pieter wondered what could have altered his partner's resolve at such a crucial point of arrest. Kellyanne realized for the first time how much she still cared for Sonny-Boy after all these years.

"What in the hell happened back there?" he said finally. "And who was that guy?"

"An old friend," she said looking down, fingers clasped in her lap. "Jonathan Pearson… We met in college… I was a sophomore at Syracuse…"

"Wait!" he said, with raised eyebrows. "Jonathan 'Sonny-Boy' Pearson? The starting quarterback?"

"One and the same," she said. "Why? You heard of him?"

"Hell yes!" he said. "Me and every fan of the New York Giant's football team! He was drafted, pulled a stint on the practice squad for a year, got cut, and was never heard from again. I guess times got hard and he made a wrong turn somewhere…"

"I'll say," she said. "Never would've thought he'd end up this way… Didn't seem like the type, you know? Clean cut, manners, and a good student… The kinda guy you'd bring home to meet your parents…"

"Sounds like the one who got away…" said Peter. "Am I close?"

She didn't answer, instead looking through the passenger window. Peter pulled to the side of the road and stopped the car abruptly. He shoved it into park, cut off the engine, and turned to look at her.

"Is that what this was all about?" he said, with a voice an octave below a scream. "You dropped your guard while reminiscing? Kellyanne, you could've been killed back there!"

She turned to look at him. Tears rolled down her cheeks.

"You don't think I know that, Peter?" she said, clenching her teeth and slamming her right fist into the palm of her left hand. "I'm not the fucking iceberg everyone thinks I am… I have feelings too… And a job like this makes it difficult to deal with the fact that I've lost every man I ever cared about!" She leaned forward, burying her face in both hands.

Several minutes passed. Peter reached for her left shoulder. She brushed his hand away and reached for the ignition.

"Fuck it," she said, trying to turn the inserted key.

"Let's get the hell out of here!"

"Stop," said Peter, grabbing her trembling right hand. "Stop it, Kellyanne!"

Screaming like a trapped alley cat, Kellyanne dislodged her hand and raised it to slap his face. He caught it, trapping it on his chest. She punched wildly with her free hand, which he cradled and pinned against the passenger seat. She sat silent with lips that quivered, looking into his eyes. Peter shook his head.

"I can't stand to see you like this, Kellyanne..." he whispered. "Although, you *are* the only woman I know that looks this beautiful when she cries..."

His smile forced her to do the same; the two of them breaking into simultaneous laughter.

Suddenly, a rush of irrationality hit her. Nothing mattered anymore... Nothing but this moment! She freed her right hand to find the warmth of his crotch. Peter released his belt buckle and unzipped his pants. He released her left hand, and she did the same. Before the trousers could get past his knees, Kellyanne had straddled him. She held his rock-hard member in place with her left hand and sat down, fully impaling herself.

Taking a moment to adjust to the level of sudden penetration, Kellyanne soon began to move up and down, sounding the horn with every upstroke. Grabbing a tuft of curls on both sides of his head, she stared deeply into the eyes of her redeemer. With clenched teeth, Peter raised his hips and pulled her down forcefully with every stroke. Faster and faster, their groans grew louder and louder. Kellyanne felt a shudder she hadn't felt in years. She raised both hands to beat violently against the roof.

"OH GOD! JESUS! PETER! PETER! PEEETERRR!"

"KELLYANNE! Aaahhhh!"

Peter lunged forward. Kellyanne pulled his head deep into her heaving chest, as she collapsed against the steering wheel. The horn released a long, steady proclamation into the stillness of the night...

CHAPTER

THIRTY-SEVEN

Meanwhile, across town, a red Ford F-150 pulled up to the entrance of Saks Fifth Avenue with a Dodge Ram minivan in tow. The tall, burly driver got out, put on a pair of Latex gloves, walked to the side of the van, opened the cargo door and removed a black cadaver bag. He tossed it over his right shoulder and walked around to the sidewalk. Laying the bag down just left of the entrance, he unzipped it, distributing a wallet and body parts at the door. Beginning with the head and upper body, he carefully positioned the right and left arms next to the shoulder blades, and each leg against their original sockets at the pelvic bone. He stood, scrutinized the remains, pulled a blue ribbon from his right coat pocket, and gently placed it center forehead. Finally, he straightened his back, and with two fingers touched his own forehead, heart, left and right chest.

"In the name of the Father, the Son, and the Holy Spirit," he chanted, before bringing the fingers to his lips, kissing them, and pointing at the corpse.

Moments later, he returned to the van, tossed the empty bag into the cargo compartment and closed the door. He then disconnected the hitch, threw it onto the truck's bed, closed the latch, and got into the truck. Leaning to his right for the cell phone in the passenger seat, he dialed 911.

"Yes, ma'am," he said after clearing his throat. "I want to report a dead body in front of Saks Fifth Avenue Off Fifth. It's Nellyanne Summers… Ma'am? Let's just say I'm not only a concerned citizen, I was a close acquaintance. You'll find proper identification behind her head when you arrive. May wanna notify the thirteenth police precinct… Her sister, Kellyanne, works there. She'll confirm the validity of this call…"

He hung up on the dispatcher as she continued to ask questions, tossed it at the passenger seat, grabbed the steering wheel with both hands, smiled, and drove away.

The next morning, Kellyanne woke up in Peter's apartment, swooning in a peaceful state of bliss. When she rolled to her right, Peter was sitting on the bed next to her, showered with a towel around his waist. He gently stroked her hair and smiled. She sat up, took his hand and kissed it.

"Good morning," he hummed in the key of G. "How about some breakfast before you head back? They've got great French toast at the IHOP down the street. What do you have a taste for?"

Kellyanne looked at him and smiled. "Me?" she cooed. "Well…"

She reached for the towel, gave it a big tug, looked at Peter, and slowly lowered her head…

Back at the precinct, the fresh scent of bona filled the air. The sound of drilling and hammering echoed loudly from the far end of the room. Detectives Fresno and Caine stood when Kellyanne and Peter came through the front door.

"Weren't expecting you guys in so early," said Caine. "How'd the stakeout go?"

"Went well," said Peter.

"Come up with anything?" said Fresno.

"Two kilos of rock cocaine," said Kellyanne with a big smile.

"And one dead Latin King," Peter asserted. He looked at a still smiling Kellyanne.

"Now that's a worthwhile endeavor," said Caine.

Just then, Captain Grant opened his office door. Kellyanne looked at him and pointed to the back of the room.

"What's all the commotion about, sir?" she said.

"Finishing up the new ladies' bathroom," he said. "Mayor's under pressure to hire more women…"

"Oh, well," said Kellyanne with a sigh. "Gonna miss my little private cubbyhole…But all in the name of progress." She remembered Nellyanne's account of her rendezvous there with Peter. She thought it best not to look his way right now.

Captain Grant's phone rang. When he walked into his office, Peter and Kellyanne chided the newly promoted Fresno and Caine with high-fives and verbal accolades. Moments later, Captain Grant walked out of his office. His face looked as if he'd seen a ghost.

"Got another one, folks," he said, his voice shaking noticeably. "Saks Fifth Avenue, this time. Fresno, why don't you and Caine take the lead on this one. Detective Summers, I need to see you in my office…"

"On it, Captain," said Fresno.

He and Caine summoned Deputies Barnes and Reinhold, and left the building, smiling from ear to ear.

Kellyanne looked at Peter and followed Grant into the office. Once inside, he turned around to face her. He did not offer her a seat. His eyes watered. He looked to the ceiling, then back at her, taking and holding both of her hands.

"What is it, sir?" she said. Tears began to stream down her face as she sensed the severity… the imminent pain of the moment. She'd never seen him cry before…

"Tell me! WHAT HAS HAPPENED CAPTAIN GRANT!"

"Kelly," he said, grasping her hands tightly. "I have some bad news…"

THE END